Eight Seconds to Forever

BOOK 5 OF THE MEN OF THE SPRAWLING A RANCH SERIES

BY

ANNA ALEXANDER

annaalexander.net

Newsletter

http://eepurl.com/Q0tsz

House of Rosenorn
Eight Seconds to Forever
ALL RIGHTS RESERVED

Eight Seconds to Forever © 2017 Anna Alexander
Print Edition

Edited by Gwen Hayes. Copy Edit by Eilis Flynn
Cover design by April Rickard with Dewpoint Studios
Cover photography by Studio Smexy

Print publication July 2017

Melody Webber is done with the men in her small town. Why was it so difficult to find a Mr. suitable enough to make her a Mrs.? After seeking the answers in a bottle of wine, her friend Jack Cannon not only saves her from the embarrassment of committing a party foul at a family function, the sexy cowboy shows her just how desirable she is with a night of passion she was never going to forget.

When Jack sees his good friend Melody drown her sorrows over another failed relationship, he had to prove she was more than worthy of the passion she had always desired. After tasting Mel's sweet fire, Jack's eager for another taste, but he's returning to the sport that almost killed him, and if her brother and the other hands on the ranch find out, he'd be facing nastier foes than the bulls he tangles with in the arena.

Melody agrees to keep their newfound relationship on the down low until an unplanned pregnancy blows the lid off the surprise. With a baby on the way, Melody has to decide if she can plan on a future with a baby daddy who risks his life every weekend for fame and a silver buckle, or if she needs to resettle in greener, more stable pastures.

With the clock ticking, Jack now must work his Cannon charm and convince his lady love that they can have it all.

DEDICATION

Para mi familia. Siempre.

Find Anna Online

Website
annaalexander.net

Facebook
facebook.com/pages/Anna-Alexander/282170065189471

Twitter
twitter.com/AnnaWriter

Newsletter
http://eepurl.com/Q0tsz

Chapter One

MELODY WEBBER DIDN'T know what was worse: the impending mega-sneeze threatening to blow snot all over the inside of her front door or the sight of Jerry Galloway standing on her porch with his baseball hat in his hands.

Ah, crap. Usually, she remembered to look through the peephole before answering the door, but the half-bottle of cold medicine she had downed the night before combined with the crying jag over yet another man who had turned out to be an utter disappointment had her forgetting the first rule of living alone as a single woman.

"Oh, Jerry." She wrapped the sides of her hoodie around her middle. "This is not—"

"Mel, please," he interrupted with his hand raised as a stop sign two inches from her nose. "Let's not make this any harder."

But it *was* hard. It was painfully difficult, as she knew exactly what he was going to say. It was the same thing he said every time he showed up at her door since he had fallen off the combine on his father's farm and landed on his head.

Perhaps it was best if she just let him get it over with so she could return to her cocoon of blankets and try to capture a few more minutes of sleep before she faced the wretched sunshine of another beautiful summer day.

She heaved a sigh and melted against the doorframe. "You may continue."

"Mel. You're a great girl, but I think we should break up. You're into books and culture and shit, and I like to drink beer and watch the Cougs play. We're like oil and vinegar. We don't mesh."

"Water. We're oil and water."

"Whatever. We're just not a good fit."

"Uh-huh."

Their differences had been one of the reasons why he had first asked her out, or so he claimed. And for a month, their relationship had been pretty solid. Not fireworks or an epic love story kind of hot, but nice. Steady. He was polite, a little shy, and opened doors for her when they went out.

And he was cute too, with his closely cropped blond hair and pink cheeks. He looked every bit like the All-American linebacker he had been in high school with his big shoulders and thick thighs.

Then suddenly he broke up with her. One bright morning he had showed up on her doorstep with his hat in his hands to tell her their differences were just too different.

While she had been saddened by his announcement, his change of heart hadn't been a complete surprise. Often, their dates ended up in a heavy make-out session because they ran short on conversation. Really, how much longer had she expected their relationship to last? So, it had been with an understanding but crushed spirit when she had said good-bye to Jerry.

But that had been the day before his accident and his short-term memory loss. This was now breakup, what? Twenty-one, twenty-two? With him appearing at her door every few weeks in the same fashion he had the year before, thinking they were still a couple.

The first few times, she smiled and tried to look crestfallen as he let her down gently. It was embarrassing enough to relive the breakup, let alone remind him that they had already separated and he was now going out with Stephanie Malonetti.

Stephanie Malonetti, of all people! The woman took extra delight in making Melody fall in the dunk tank at the school fundraiser every year. She was also a checker at the local grocery store and always made some snarky comment on whatever junk food Melody was purchasing.

"Snoqualmie Ice Cream and pizza rolls, Mel? Another breakup?" she'd ask, then giggle behind her hand.

Gah, how annoying.

Sometimes Jerry remembered his accident partway through his spiel and had the grace to apologize. But more recently, she learned to check the peephole and pretend she wasn't home when he stopped by.

Which was what she would have done if her head cold hadn't turned her brain to mush and she lost her ability to think straight.

"Achoo!" She sneezed and pulled a wad of tissues from her pocket. "Sorry, Jerry. Look, I understand. I'm a little bit country, and you're a whole lotta country."

"I know this is a big shock," he interrupted. "But believe me. This is for the best."

Really? Good God, man, open your ears.

"You're right. Thank you for opening my eyes. Good luck with your future endeavors. Thanks for stopping by."

"Wow." He blinked with palpable relief. "Geez, Mel. Thanks for being a peach about this." He settled his cap on his head and shot her a big goofy grin. "I know the perfect guy for you is out there. Catch you later."

"Right." She blew her nose and gave him a half-hearted smile as he bounded down the stairs.

The perfect guy is out there.

Ha. That had been her mantra for far too long. At this point, her social life more resembled those of the schoolteachers of the Wild West. Back when teachers were not only allowed to marry, they were forbidden from even fraternizing with the other sex while employed.

Boy, had times changed. Now her students were offering up their recently divorced uncles and fathers as potential date bait.

How sad was that? Her single status was so well known, even her sixth-grade students were trying to hook her up.

"Stupid. This is so stupid," she muttered and shuffled toward the kitchen to fix a cup of tea.

Jerry's visit was the salt rubbed into a wound caused by yet another demise of a promising relationship the night before. At times, she had to believe Cupid visited Bacchus and had one drink too many before he lobbed an arrow at her suitors. That little cherubic brat was missing the mark every time.

Thankfully it was Saturday, and all she wanted was to finish that chocolate cream pie that she had intended on sharing with her date and snuggle in bed to watch marathons of home improvement shows on HGTV.

Or not, she realized as she spotted the brightly wrapped package with the profusion of yellow curling ribbon sitting on the kitchen table.

Right. The baby shower.

Ugh. She loved her family, loved them more than anything. But the temptation to bail and call out sick for the party was making her itch to reach for the phone.

Of course, her family being as spectacular as they were,

would allow her to stay home with nothing but well wishes and promises to bring over buckets of soup. But there was no way she could miss baby Marta's welcome home party.

Greta and Trey's baby had arrived in the world a few weeks prior, but they had wanted to wait until they held her in their arms before holding any type of baby shower. The loss of their son was never far from their thoughts, and the pair had understandably developed a few superstitions. Even with their new baby nestled safely in their arms, Melody saw the stress of worry eating away at her friends. It was in the tremble of their lips and the light in their eyes every time they looked at their daughter. Hopefully, in time, their concern would cease enough to allow them to enjoy their little girl to the fullest. But she knew to tell them not to worry was as effective and as arrogant as telling the sun not to shine.

To miss out on the baby's official welcome was going to be one of those moments she'd regret forever. And Marta couldn't care less if her Aunty Melody was having an extended rocky patch in her social life. It was time to pull on her French-cut bikini briefs and be the modern sophisticated woman she pretended to be.

She found a few more decongestants underneath the hair bands and copious tubes of travel toothpaste she accrued from her dentist in the bathroom drawer and washed the pills down with a sip of water before dragging herself into the shower, determined to cleanse herself of any negativity from the last twenty-four hours.

The simple routine of washing and primping helped to keep her mind focused on the present and the way her blood circulated through her body. By the time she left the house two hours later in her favorite light-pink sundress and strappy gold sandals, she felt more like her old self.

Old? No no no. Not *old*, but old as in her usual chipper self. *Right, girl. Get on with your bad self.*

Upon driving down the lane toward the main house on the Sprawling A Ranch, the profusion of balloons decorating the front porch added to the lift in her spirits.

Rafe Montoya, or as she pronounced his name in her mind *Rrrrrafeal*, paused outside of the horse barn and waved at her as she parked her car.

Just looking at the sexy Latino still had the ability to make her heart thud and cause a fine sheen of sweat to gather over her upper lip. Especially since she knew what he looked like underneath that cotton T-shirt and tight jeans. The man was golden skin from head to toe.

Many a night she wondered what would have been if she and Rafe had continued dating. But when her fantasies ran to completion, she knew that her time with Rafe had taught her that even though you were physically attracted to a person, if the emotional spark wasn't there, the connection would never take hold.

Pity. He was quite delicious.

"Hey, Mel," he said as she climbed out of the car. "We've been wondering where you been."

"I've had a slow start. Besides, I'm not that late."

He pressed a kiss to her cheek. "Good to see you."

"Nice to see you, too." She gestured to the balloons. "Did Trey buy out every party store in the city?"

"Just about." He chuckled. "He had to rent a U-Haul truck to get them all here."

Together they walked around to the back of the house where they followed the sound of laughter and Ben playing guitar. On every picnic table and lawn chair, more balloons bobbed in the breeze.

"Melody," Greta called out from her seat under the newly constructed gazebo, complete with ceiling fan. In her arms napped a tiny bundle of pink blanket and baby. "We were wondering where you've been. Date went well, I take it?" she asked under her breath with an added eyebrow wiggle as Melody drew near.

"Date went not at all," she replied, keeping a safe, germ-free distance from mom and baby.

"Oh, no," Greta mourned. "What happened?"

"I'll fill you in later. It's probably for the best." She waved her hand as if everything was easy breezy and she hadn't spent the better part of the night crying her eyes out. "I'd give you a hug, but I've been fighting a head cold or allergies and don't want to get the baby sick by standing too close. Actually, maybe I should just go home."

"No. Stay. It's not a party without you here. And I'm going to put Marta down for a proper nap soon anyway. The coolers are filled with beer and wine, but there's some ginger ale in the refrigerator."

"Thanks. I'll check it out."

She blew a kiss in the direction of the baby and turned, stopping short with a gasp when she almost ran into an older woman who had come up behind her. She had bright white hair and was dressed in a yellow cardigan sweater.

"Sorry, Melody," the woman said. "Didn't mean to sneak up on you like that."

"That's all right, Mrs. O'Neal. How are you? And congratulations. Grandmotherhood looks good on you."

"Thanks, sweetie. Jim and I are just pleased as punch." She gestured at Greta's father, who was chatting with Trey as well as Melody's brother, Mark, across the yard.

"Are you staying in town long?"

"Jim heads back in a few days for work, but I get to stay for a few weeks with this little bundle of preciousness." She tickled the baby's cheek, who squirmed with a smile in return.

Melody squelched the flair of jealousy over the fact that the little bundle of preciousness wasn't hers and forced a smile. Motherhood had always been in the master plan of her life, and now that she was approaching thirty, the emptiness in her arms grew more pronounced every day. "Well… I'm just going to put this present with the others."

"Oh, Melody." Mrs. O'Neal stopped her. "Did I hear you were still single?"

"Yes?" she replied, suddenly fearful of the delight in Mrs. O'Neal's eyes.

"Wonderful." She clapped her hands. "Just the other day, I met my friend Shelly's bird man. Greta, you remember my friend Shelly who I go to the casino with on Wednesdays."

"Yes, Mother."

"Anyway, her bird man is just adorable. And he's single," she sang at the end.

Melody blinked and shook her head. Apparently, the cold medicine she took earlier was affecting her hearing. "I'm sorry. Bird man?"

"Yes. Shelly had some birds roosting in her chimney, and they were causing quite the mess. So she called a service to come get them, and they sent Toby. Or is his name Tyler?"

"He's an exterminator?" Melody asked, still trying to get a grasp on the conversation.

"No, no." Mrs. O'Neal waved her hands. "He's more in the animal control business. Not that there's anything wrong about being an exterminator. There was a show on cable about an exterminator a while ago that was fascinating, but I digress. You see, the best part is he's moving out to Yakima. That's so close to Mission, you'll practically be neighbors. So, what do you say? Can I give him your number?"

"Mother, he's a stranger," Greta groaned with a wince. "No, you can't give him her number."

"Oh, please. A stranger is just a friend you haven't met yet."

"Or a serial killer."

"Let me think on it, Mrs. O'Neal," Melody interrupted. "I'll let you know."

"Please do. You're too pretty to be single."

"Mother!"

"What?"

Melody left mother and daughter to bicker the merits of strangers and the plight of the modern woman in the era of Craigslist killers and misogynistic bastards multiplying like mold spores and escaped toward the house, taking a brief detour to add the present she brought to the mountain stacked on the picnic table.

Goose bumps raced up her arms as she stepped into the cool air-conditioned interior of the main house and followed the sounds of laughter through the mudroom and into the kitchen.

"Hey, Melody. There you are," Faith greeted her as she entered. She lifted a bowl piled high with various types of cut melon. "Ta-da!"

"Good for you," Melody replied and rummaged through the refrigerator until she found the bottle of ginger ale. "Now when are you going to actually make something that requires a stove? You said your cooking lessons were going well."

"They are. But I don't know if I'm ready to jump into the frying pan for a family function yet."

"We believe in you, Faith," Melody's sister-in-law Gabriella reassured her as she drew a piping-hot casserole dish from the oven. "Why don't you take over on the salmon?"

The redhead's eyes boggled. "*The* salmon? As in the only fish recipe these cowboys will eat?"

Gabriella patted her on the shoulder. "You can do it. It's a breeze. Especially since the fish has been marinating for a few hours and now all you have to do is put it on the grill and make sure it doesn't burn."

The crooked set of Faith's lips suggested she wasn't reassured.

"Will you be with me the whole time?" she asked.

"The whole time." Gabriella made a cross-sign over her heart.

"Okay." Faith rolled her shoulders and shadow boxed with her hands. "I can do this."

"And you." Gabriella turned to Melody with her finger pointed. "Spill it. How did your date go last night?"

Melody rolled her eyes and jumped up to sit on the huge kitchen table. "It didn't."

"What?" Both women gasped.

"What happened?" Gabriella asked. "I thought things were going so well with you two."

"So did I." Melody shrugged and smoothed the hem of her skirt over her knees. "First he texted to confirm what time our date was. Then twenty minutes later came the text saying he was running late. Then came the text saying he was running *really* late. Then he didn't show at all."

"What a jackass," Gabriella said and Faith nodded. "What is it with men these days? Are they all assholes or just the young ones?"

"Oh, don't get me started about dating someone younger than me," Melody said with a sigh. "I'm already scraping the bottom of the barrel of eligible men here in town. And it doesn't help that Miss Greedy-pants here has *two* men."

Faith blinked at her with surprise. "You wanted to date Colby or Ben?"

"No." Melody stuck out her tongue and shuddered. "I know them too well." She sighed again. "You just look so happy. I want some of that for myself."

"They do make me happy," Faith said with a dreamy smile on her lips. "Who was your date with last night? Chase? Who is he again?"

"The new foreman at the Benedictos' farm."

"Oh. I thought the foreman was named Corey."

"No. Corey was the construction guy I went out with a few months ago."

"What happened to him?"

"Ex-con."

"Really," Gabriella gasped. "I didn't hear that. For what?"

"He said DUI," Melody replied. "But it sounded like he served an awful lot of prison time for a first offense. Or so he claimed."

"Wait." Faith lifted her hand. "Why do I remember a 'John'?"

Melody's right eye twitched as she remembered. "John was at the beginning of the year. Two dates and he disappeared. It was as if he never existed."

"Wow." Gabriella popped a grape in her mouth and dropped her hand on her hip as she shook her head. "You've had quite a crappy year, haven't you?"

Preach, sista. Preach.

"I don't know." Melody glanced down and contemplated the bubbles in her glass of soda as they popped up to the surface. "I think it's this town. At least that's what my theory is because I believe I'm a good person and a joy to be with."

"Oh, you are." The girls agreed with vigorous nods.

Melody tapped her fingernail on the side of her glass and confessed to the plan she had been ruminating on every time one of her relationships flamed out like a bottle rocket. "I've been thinking." She sucked in a breath. "I've been thinking that maybe I should widen my dating pool."

"Of course," Gabriella said and added little serving spoons to the plate of condiments. "There are only so many single men in Mission, and if you add Yakima and Ellensburg, there still isn't a lot to choose from."

"I'm thinking of even further away," Melody said. "Like the city."

"The city? You want to try a long-distance relationship?"

"No," and she drew the word out with a long *o*. "With the economy improving, knock on wood," she added with a rap of her knuckles on the tabletop, "more districts are passing levies to build more schools and hire teachers. I'm thinking of applying."

"You want to move across the mountains?" Greta screeched from the doorway to the kitchen. "Since when? What for? What did I miss?"

"I was saying that I've been giving some thought about maybe moving to where there are more opportunities for me to grow." Melody sighed and her lip curled as if she bit down on a plug of ginger. "I don't want to be the spinster schoolteacher. I want a family of my own, but at the same time, I don't want to settle. I don't think Mr. Right is within a forty-mile radius."

"Screw what I said to my mother earlier," Greta said. "I'm getting the name of that exterminator."

Melody chuckled and waved her hands for Greta to stop. "Let's not go to extremes. I haven't submitted any job applications. Yet."

"Well, don't." Greta joined her at the table then blew out a breath. "No. Don't listen to me. I'm being selfish. You're my best friend, and I can't bear to think of you being more than twenty minutes away."

Melody patted Greta on the back of the hand. "As I said. It's just an idea."

"What's an idea?" Mark asked as he entered the kitchen. "And what's the holdup on the food?"

"I was debating what type of BDSM gear to get you for your birthday," Melody replied. "We've all heard how much you love being tied up." She flashed her brother a cheeky grin.

"Smartass," he muttered. He kissed his wife on the cheek and reached for the platter of hamburger patties in her hands.

"Need some help, Faith?" Gabriella asked. "The salmon is in the fridge. Don't look so scared. You can carry a platter of fish."

"All right." Faith removed the treasured fillets from the refrigerator while Melody contributed by retrieving a bowl of potato salad in one hand while carrying her ginger ale in the other.

Set up underneath the tent that had been erected to afford some shade from the blazing August sun was a feast for the masses. Unlike their damp cousins on the west side of the Cascade Mountains, summers in Central Washington were dry and scorching hot with constant temperatures in the high 90s. The neighboring town of Yakima was so balmy, it even had the nickname of the Palm Springs of Washington.

"Man," Adam said as Melody set down the potato salad. "It's about time. I am starving."

His girlfriend Nicolette handed him a plate. "You're always starving."

"Maybe it's because I can't wait to get to the dessert part. And what comes after dessert." He gave her a playful slap on the backside.

"Watch yourself, Maguire. Or I'll go east coast on ya."

"Oh yeah," Melody said. "How was the trip to New York?"

Boyfriend and girlfriend shared a secretive glance.

"Great," Nic replied with hearts in her eyes.

"Better than great," Adam amended and leaned forward to give her a kiss.

Ack. Young love. Could the two of them be any cuter?

"Is that a new necklace?" Greta asked Nic. "Did you get that from a street vendor on your trip? I have an aunt who only buys her jewelry from street vendors and at art fairs."

"Oh." Nicolette adjusted the collar of her shirt to cover up the chain. "No. It's an old piece."

"Was that a charm on the end? Or a pendant?" As a jewelry designer, Greta was like Gollum with their precious when it came to shiny objects.

Nic glanced around as her cheeks turned pink. "Neither?"

"Is it beaded? Are the beads handmade like mine?"

Adam started to laugh. "Just show her, darlin'. They're gonna find out sooner or later."

"I guess so." Nic sighed and pulled the chain from her shirt. "But we were going to wait before we said anything."

Dangling on the end of the gold chain, a diamond ring caught the sun and sparkled in a cloud of shimmery rainbows.

"Nic and I are getting hitched," Adam announced and hugged his girl against his side. Nic's usual bemused smirk was replaced by a shy smile that stretched from ear to ear.

Friends and family erupted into cheers, startling the sleeping Marta nearby, who burst into cries over having her nap disrupted.

Melody wobbled on her feet as if a weight had slammed into her chest and stumbled back on shaky legs. Joy and sadness brought tears to her eyes as a war waged within her over being excited for her friends or being incredibly depressed.

What was wrong with her? She loved Adam like a brother. And Nicolette had become a good friend over the past few months. But the sight of their obvious happiness was a dagger to her heart.

Was it ever going to be her turn? Was she ever going to find the one who looked at her with so much love, it reached out and grabbed you by the throat?

The glass in her hand felt as if it had suddenly gained twenty pounds and it dropped, spilling its contents onto the lawn. As she gazed unseeing into the distance, a bit of red caught her eye. She blinked the image into focus and recognized the giant cooler that stored more beverages.

She stumbled over and lifted the lid, revealing bottles of beer that sat like hidden treasure amongst the cubes of ice. Along the side were several bottles of white wine, one of which was already opened. With a little celebratory shout, she lifted out the bottle and was happy to see that it was mostly full and yanked the cork out with her teeth. She filled a red plastic cup to the rim and tucked the bottle under her arm before she crossed to a nearby lawn chair and flopped onto the plastic weaving.

"Let's hear it for the happy couple," Trey announced.

As the cheers went up, Melody lifted her glass in salute then took a healthy swallow.

Chapter Two

"MELODY? THERE YOU are. Everyone's been looking for you."

She lifted her eyelids just enough to make out the lanky figure of Jack Cannon standing in the doorway to her hideout.

Technically, her hideout was Greta's workroom where she made the beaded jewelry she sold online, but for Melody's immediate needs, it was a room with a twin bed and no noise.

"What's up?" she slurred.

Jack sighed and pressed some numbers on his phone. "Hey, Mark, I found her. She's—" He broke off as she struggled to sit up and gestured with her hands for him to stop talking.

"She's…waving at me?" he asked with a confused wrinkle on his brow.

Melody's eyes bulged and she scowled, making the cut motion across her throat with arms that felt as if they were made of Jell-O.

"I don't know," he said. "She's your sister."

"Tell him to mind his own business," she instructed with a huff.

"You heard that, right?" Jack smiled. "She's fine. Yeah. I'll call you if we need you."

"What do you want?" she asked and clutched at her spinning head.

"Ah, darlin'." He squatted before her and rested his hands on her knees. "You don't look so good."

"You're no prize yourself."

Lie. Such a lie and you know it.

"I'm sorry." She reached out to touch his cheek and her hand flopped at the wrist to land on his shoulder. "You're adorable. You know you're adorable."

His smile widened, showing off his even, white teeth. How he managed to keep all of them in his head after the years spent riding bulls was beyond her.

Well, maybe his teeth survived, but his time spent in the saddle hadn't completely spared his boyish good looks. A scar in the shape of a tiny tuning fork bisected his right eyebrow, and another scar was a pink slash just under his chin. And who knew how many times he had broken his nose.

Yet, with all of those seeming imperfections, they only added to Jack's bad-boy allure. The man was a lady-killer with a trail of broken hearts left all over the west.

"And you're intoxicated, Ms. Webber." He plucked an empty wine bottle off the floor and examined the label. "So that's what happened to the Chateau Ste. Michelle. Mrs. O'Neal was wondering where it went."

"It went to a good home, that's where. Oh." She clutched at her middle as the sensation of a million minuscule hands crawled up her throat and tickled her uvula. "Please move," she pleaded in a pained whisper.

"Uh-oh. I've seen that look many times." Jack stood up and searched the room, coming up with a wastepaper bin from beneath the desk.

"Jack," she moaned and reached for the bin, catching it

under her chin a second before the entire contents of her stomach came out to say hello.

That's it. Barf in front of the cute guy. The perfect capper to an absolutely shitty day.

"Go away, Jack," she groaned between heaves. "Just leave me."

Leave me alone with my misery as I wallow in the consequences of my immature decision to drink my troubles away.

"Sit tight, darlin'."

His booted feet shuffled out of her line of sight, and she hung her head over the ruined basket as her stomach tried to follow him out of the room.

He returned in a few short moments and sat beside her on the bed, and then ran his palm up and down her back. "That's it, darlin'. Get all of that liquor out."

"Are you holding my hair back?" she asked, trying to look up at him.

"Well, yeah. You have nice hair, and I'd hate for it to get all icky."

"Oh." His cute little face blurred as tears fell down her cheeks. "Thanks."

The trickle of tears soon turned into full-on sobs. Man, she was messed up.

"Shit, Mel. Maybe I should get Mark or one of the girls."

"No." She held out her hand. "I've just—I've just had a really bad—" month, year, lifetime—"day. Sorry you have to witness my downfall."

"No problem, sweetheart. That's what friends are for. Here." He handed her a wet washcloth that had been creating a damp spot on his jeans.

"Thanks, Jack. Ugh. What a mess." She wiped her face and hands and then stood, the offending bucket held out in front of her as if it were about to explode.

Jack followed her into the bathroom. "Can I get you anything? Water? Ginger ale?"

"No. I'll be fine."

"Let me at least grab some toothpaste from Trey and Greta's bathroom."

Before she could protest, he dashed away, and she tried to clean up as best as she could. Even though she rinsed out the waste bin, she made a mental note to buy a replacement. She couldn't in good conscience put it back for Greta to use.

As she was leaning over the sink, rinsing her mouth, a tube of toothpaste appeared before her.

"Here you go, sweetheart."

She mumbled a "thank you" and used her finger to brush her teeth.

"How are you feeling?" he asked as she dried her hands on a towel.

"Better. I just really want to go home and crawl into bed." *Where I will stay for the next thirty years.*

"Let me drive you home."

"Oh, I don't want to take you away from the party."

He lifted her chin with his finger. "One, I'd feel better if I knew that you got home safely. And two, the party is just all of us that live here. We're together all the time. The only difference is now there's a new little person and a crap ton of balloons. Next weekend, we'll have a cookout and we'll be doing the same things we are now."

Wasn't that the truth. Over the past year, Trey had found all sorts of holidays and excuses to throw a party. Melody's favorites had been National Chocolate Chip Day and Something on a Stick Day. Who knew that skewering a pineapple and roasting it over an open fire with some rum and coconut could be so fun? Hazardous, but fun. And Adam's eyebrows did grow back.

"If you're absolutely positive it's not going to put you out."

"It'll be fine," he said. "Let's go."

She said her good-byes to Greta and her brother, who let her go with a frown and a gruff order to call him when she got home, and waved at the rest of the crew before finally being allowed to leave with a plate of cake and a bowl of potato salad.

Jack escorted her to his beat-up Silverado and opened the passenger door with a flourish.

"Oh, wait a second," he said and retrieved an old saddle blanket from the toolbox on the flatbed. He took the blanket and shook the wool free from dust and straw before laying it across the torn seat. "Don't want you to snag your dress there."

She contained a giggle. He was being quite gentlemanly. "I appreciate the thought."

Jack's Silverado had been the brunt of many jokes on the ranch. The color was more primer than paint, and the front headlight was strapped onto the grill with zip ties. She wouldn't be surprised if the muffler was attached with duct tape.

But Jack loved his truck. He raved about his truck. And the smile on his face as he slid behind the wheel made her forgive him for having her sit on a dusty blanket that smelled of horse and alfalfa.

"You look better," he said. "At least you're no longer as white as a ghost."

"I'm sober now," she replied. "Unfortunately."

"So what's been going on? What's got you so sad, pretty lady?"

She gazed out of the window at the vast acres of empty pasture and was reminded of her equally barren social life.

Turning back to Jack, she sighed and said, "Man troubles.

It's always man troubles. I don't understand. Why am I so undateable? What's wrong with me that makes men not want to go out with me?"

Jack's eyes widened in that deer-in-the-headlights-of-a-Mack-truck way. His mouth dropped open as if to answer before he snapped it shut and drew in a breath.

"There's nothing wrong with you," he finally replied in a voice that reminded her of a balloon with a slow leak of air.

"Liar," she said. "You had a look in your eye, and you stopped yourself from answering. What were you thinking?"

He snuck a quick glance her way before looking back on the road as he chuckled.

"You're smart." He wagged his finger at her. "That's what I was going to say. You're smart. You're *really* smart. Almost too smart."

"Too smart? Are you kidding me? I'm not datable because I'm smart? What does that even mean?"

"I'm going to be honest with you, Melody. Can I be honest?"

"Oh, please do." This should be good.

"Keep in mind this is only my opinion as that of a man of this world. All right?"

"Gotcha."

"I think you are just too much."

The Silverado clipped along the country lane back into town at a steady pace as she waited for him to continue.

And...

"Please tell me there is more to your statement than that."

He laughed. "Look at yourself, Mel. You're beautiful, you're smart. You have a good career. Stuff like that can be intimidating to a man. They can't pull anything over on you, you'll catch them in a lie. They can't provide for you, 'cuz you're doing that for yourself. What else is there for a guy to offer you?"

"Oh, I don't know. How about some love and attention?" Duh. "Why is it a bad thing that I can provide for myself?"

"It's not a bad thing. Men—well, let's face it. Men are pretty stupid. And basic. We want to be made to feel like we are the king of the world, the great conqueror. That we can do anything. And when faced with a woman that can probably do it better than us, it's a challenge we don't know how to win. So we tend to stick with that which is familiar. Needy women."

"I don't know if that's the most brilliant thing I've ever heard or the lamest."

He grinned and shot her a wink. "Probably right on both accounts." He reached out and squeezed her thigh in commiseration before putting his hand back on the wheel.

"So, what? I'm supposed to play stupid?"

"No. Of course not. Don't change who you are. Mel, the guy who was meant to be with you, he's got to be pretty spectacular, because you're pretty spectacular. Don't settle for anything less. Don't worry. The guy for you is out there somewhere."

Out there somewhere.

And again, the thought of moving to the city crossed her mind. If she stayed in Mission, she'd probably never find the man for her.

They neared the center of town and her neighborhood when a sign caught her eye.

"Oh my God," she shouted. "Pull over. Pull over, Jack."

"What's wrong?" He shot her a panic-stricken look. "Are you going to hurl in my truck?"

"No, no. Look."

Down a small lane lined by poplar trees sat a two-story Victorian home. The orange and pink of the setting sun bathed the wood siding that had seen better days in a soft fairy-like glow.

The white paint was so chipped, it was even missing from entire slats.

Despite the weathered appearance, Melody loved that house. She loved the huge wrap-around front porch and the turret on the corner. She loved the gingerbread trim and big bay windows in the front. But most especially, she longed to sit on the captain's walk on the roof and look out on the valley while she snuggled next to the man of her dreams.

The house had been built in the late 1800s by one of Mission's founding families. Over the years, the family's children and grandchildren had moved on to the city, and later generations began to sell off parts of the farm until there was only the one-acre lot left and the great, big, glorious house that more resembled a haunted mansion than a home for a modern family.

And that was what Melody found the most appealing about the house. The uniqueness, the grandeur, the romanticism of the entire era the home had been created in. A time when families spoke to each other face-to-face and people weren't glued to an electronic device twenty-four/seven.

Since the last time she had driven past the property, something new had been added to the yard. Something that gave her hope and severe disappointment in one blow.

"It's the old Emmert house," Jack said. "Am I missing something?"

"Are you kidding?" She pointed to the big sign hanging from a post on the road's edge. "It's for sale."

"Oh." He scratched at his cheek and laid his arm along the back of the seat. "I thought it was condemned a long time ago."

"No. The Hadleys bought the home six years ago when Mr. Hadley became VP at the cannery. They had begun to remodel it when he was arrested for embezzling from the cannery, and then the house fell into the bank's hands. They must have settled something for it to be back on the market."

"How do you know so much about the Hadleys?"

"I'm a teacher." She shrugged. "Stories about almost every family pass through the halls of the middle school. It's the age where parents believe their children are too young to understand what's going on, when in reality their kids are absorbing everything. But it's also the age when kids haven't learned to filter and will share, whether they're realizing it or not."

"I guess so. I don't know. I've always been on the quiet side when it came to feelings and what not. I can shoot the shit with anyone about anything, but when it comes to family business, I'll keep it in unless absolutely necessary. Know what I mean?"

"Yeah."

To outsiders, Jack was all charm and flirty cowboy, to the point one would think he never had a cloud darken his day. But Jack had suffered so many struggles in his life and faced them all with his charmingly crooked smile. To those he considered family, he lowered his guard and allowed the sensitive, reflective man to shine. Melody found that man more attractive than the brash rodeo champ, but both were pretty hunky.

She sighed and rolled down the window to prop her arms on the door and rested her chin in her hand, watching the peachy glow of sunset turn into the lavender of twilight.

"Can you imagine it, Jack? Once it's all cleaned up and renovated, spending afternoons on the porch with a glass of lemonade and a book. Or having it all lit up at Christmas time?"

"Putting up all those lights sounds like a crap ton of work."

"Geez, Jack. You're no fun."

He laughed and pushed on her shoulder. "I'm joking. Mostly. The way you describe it makes it sound real nice."

"Ugh." She turned away and curled into a ball. "Take me home, please. The longer I look, the more I want that house."

"Why don't you grab a flyer and see how much it is?"

"Why torture myself? I can't afford a down payment. I still have a few more years of student loans to pay off."

Besides, living in a house that large would only magnify her single status.

"Poor girl." He turned the truck back onto the road. "Someday soon, Mel, all of your dreams are gonna come true. I know it."

Arguments to the contrary flared along her tongue, but she knew it would be childish to voice them. Jack was being a friend and trying to cheer her up. She was sober enough to recognize the effort and not be whiny about her lack of prospects.

The rest of the ride was filled with the radio playing 1980s classic country tunes and Jack's humming. His warm baritone was so soothing, the anxiety she had carried most of the day began to dissipate and her muscles relaxed as she melted into the seat. When he pulled into her driveway, she almost asked him to keep driving just so she could remain in their cozy little cocoon for a moment longer.

"Thanks for bringing me home," she said and reluctantly climbed out of the truck.

Jack moved to follow. "I'll see you in."

"You've already done so much. And I'm fine. I'm sober now, and only a little melancholy."

"Well…" He scratched his chin. "If it's all right with you, I was hoping to catch the last half of the Mariners' game. Adam talks so much shit during the games, I'd like to watch it in some peace and quiet."

"Okay. Well, I guess you can stay. As a thank-you. Just please ignore the mess."

"You do know I live with Adam and Rafe, right? I'm sure your house is pristine in comparison."

She unlocked the door to the little two-story house she had been renting since her college days and ushered Jack inside.

Her best friend Gina had been her roommate when she signed her first lease, and the two of them had blazed a trail of laughs and good times on the short commute from Mission to Central Washington University in Ellensburg. Greta was Gina's cousin and had lived with them during her temp job teaching at the university until she met and married Trey.

Then it was Gina who got married and moved to Portland, leaving Melody alone in a house decorated much the same as when she had been a fresh-faced eighteen-year-old ready to take on the world. She set her keys on the table she had bought from IKEA and painted to look like an antique. The couch and loveseat were those she had inherited from her mother when she moved across the mountains, and mounted on the wall was the shadowbox Gina had made for her lined with all the shot glasses they had collected during her twenty-first birthday trip to Las Vegas.

"Can I get you anything to drink?" she asked her guest. "I think I have a Corona left from one of my dates. Or I have water or a diet soda."

"A pop would be great." He eyed the plate of cake she held. "Are you gonna eat that?"

The hopeful light in his eyes was so darn adorable, she handed him the plate with a sigh. "Let me get us some forks."

She was generous but not stupid. Nic made a damn fine cake. Tummy ache or no, she wasn't going to let an entire slice escape without a taste.

Jack made himself at home on the couch, pulling off his boots before setting his feet on the coffee table. "Yes! We're ahead. Way to go, Ms."

"Ah. Now I see why you wanted to hide your blue and gray."

She handed him his drink and a fork and settled in beside him. "Adam would be on you for sure. He bleeds red and blue."

"Don't know why he's such a Rangers fan."

"His brother Scott went to school in Texas and he loved his brother. He's loyal that way. And we love that about Adam."

"True. See, I told you you're a smart cookie."

They clinked their forks together in a toast then fought over the icing as they watched the Mariners battle the Rangers for the division lead.

"For a girl who was green to the gills over an hour ago, you're eating like a champ," Jack noted and swiped the last bite of cake.

Perhaps it was time, or maybe it was his company, but she felt a million times better than she had earlier. Even her sinuses appeared to have cleared up.

She knocked his feet off the table and set the plate and utensils down. "I feel better. Both inside and out. Thanks."

"My pleasure. Come here." He raised his arm and gestured for her to snuggle against his side.

As she settled into place, she realized it was the first time she and Jack had hung out together on their own. Oh, they'd been friends for years and had shared many jokes and nights out with their friends. But never had it just been the two of them, alone, for an undetermined amount of time. It was nice.

Real nice.

His muscular body was toasty-warm against hers, sending little vibrations to tickle up and down her skin. Unable to resist, she stuck her nose against his neck to inhale his manly scent. "You smell good. Why do I recognize that aftershave?"

"It's Old Spice."

"Oh yeah. My grandpa used to wear Old Spice."

"Figured." He chuckled. "My grandpa did, too. That's why I

wear it. He told me that girls love their grandpas, therefore they'll love a man who reminds them of him."

"That's pretty sneaky, Cannon."

"But effective."

"Is that how you landed Stacy the witch? Her grandfather struck me as a fan of the freshly minted money kind of fragrance."

"Nope. Stacy said it was my tight jeans and large hands she was first attracted to."

"Really? I never noticed. Besides, I thought it was the size of a man's feet we were supposed to take notice of. And yours look pretty small for a man." She knocked against his knees, urging him to remove said feet from the table again. "Must be from wearing those boots for so many years."

"I can prove different." He spread his fingers and covered her face with the entirety of his hand. "Is this big enough for you?"

She giggled and slapped at his hand, cuddling up against his side and wrapping her arm around his lean waist. "Jury's still out."

He laughed with her and hugged her tight as the Mariners ended the eighth inning with a two-run lead.

"Giddy-up, rodeo fans," said the announcer of the commercial on the television. "Tickets on sale now for the Ellensburg Rodeo. Come see the country's best riders, ropers, and barrel racers on Labor Day Weekend."

Beneath her cheek, Jack held his breath and his arm around her shoulders tensed. His entire body followed suit, and it felt as if he turned to stone in her arms. Alarm had her responding in kind, and she felt the hairs on her arm stand on end. Glancing up, she saw a deep furrow in his brow, and his lips compress and release as if he were arguing with himself.

It had been, what, three years since he sustained the injury that ended his bull riding career? Although he now walked with a minimal limp, watching his reaction to the advertisement told her the wounds seemed to still cut deep.

"Jack?" She placed her hand on the center of his chest.

"What?" He blinked at her as if waking from a dream. "Sorry. Didn't mean to zone out like that."

"I'm sorry I can't stop the rodeo announcements."

"Oh, no. No." He grabbed her hand and held it in his, cradling it against his sternum. "That's not it. I was thinking." He glanced away and worried his lip for a moment before turning to her with that frown back on his forehead. "Can you keep a secret?"

"Depends. Who did you kill and where did you hide the body?"

His trademark grin stole across his lips and her heart did a little somersault. "No body. I'm—I'm…" He licked at his lips. "I'm going back to the rodeo."

"What?" She sat up straight. "You're leaving the ranch?"

"Not entirely. I contacted the circuit, and they said I could come back and work as a pickup man. I'll be starting off at some of the smaller shows, like Bremerton or in Idaho. If I can keep up and the crowd likes me, and the competitors like me, I have a chance of going all the way to nationals. But that will take me a few years before I get to that level."

Pickup man. She remembered Gina's cousin had worked as a pickup man. Those were the fellas who rode on horseback during the show and herded the animals away from fallen cowboys. "So you won't be riding bulls?"

"No. Thought about it. I'm not ready for that level of competition. My physical therapist thinks I could all right, and I was all ready to stage a comeback when Gabriella's ex set that plan back." He rubbed at the scar over his eyebrow with his finger the same way he did every time anyone mentioned the attack when Gabriella's ex-husband and his friends kidnapped Gabriella and beat the crap out of Jack, who had tried to stop them. He had spent three days in the hospital with broken ribs, broken nose, and several lacerations as well as some internal damage. He was fortunate he survived at all.

"Does Trey know?" she asked.

"He knows I was considering it and that I've been talking with the circuit about my options. I just got the phone call yesterday. They want me to head out next weekend."

"Well, that's great," she said, already missing the time he would be away.

The two of them always had a good time together teasing her brother during the weekly barbecues on the ranch.

"Being a pickup man is a good thing? Right?" she asked, not knowing if the position was considered a demotion of any kind.

"Yeah. Yeah." The sparkle returned to his eyes, and he shifted in his seat, leaning forward with excitement. "Look, I love working on the ranch. But the rodeo is in my blood. My granddad rode in the Turquoise Circuit. My mom was a barrel racer. My dad worked with stock contractors. I've been around bulls my whole life. When I got hurt, being around that lifestyle and not being able to participate was more painful than the actual injury." He glanced away and ruffled the hair over his ear. "I thought if I moved away from all that, away from Pendleton, that pain would ease. It didn't. Only changed it a bit. I know I can't reclaim my former glory days." He grinned. "But maybe just being a part of the show will fill that hole a little."

"Well, then I wish you the best of luck. Very few people get to do what they love. And you know we'll all be there to cheer you on."

"Thanks." His brash smile turned shy. "To be honest, I'm a little nervous. Starting so late in the season. But I just got the clearance from the doc a few weeks ago. Had to sign up my memberships again and everything. There was a lot of paperwork to get together."

"You'll be great. I know it." On impulse, she leaned into him and gave him a big hug, brushing her lips against his lightly whiskered cheek.

When she pulled back, Jack was gazing at her with a bit of confusion in his eyes. He lifted his hand and brushed his thumb over her cheek, pushing her hair back over her ear.

"What?" she asked, suddenly uncertain. In the last few seconds there was a definite change in the atmosphere.

"You," he replied softly.

"Me?"

He chuckled and brushed his thumb over her cheek again. "Yeah, you. How could you ever... You just don't know, do you?"

The confusion in his eyes turned into resolve. The line of his jaw tightened and his nostrils flared ever so slightly. A blink of an eye later, he settled his mouth over hers in a kiss that stole her breath.

What the hell?

Chapter Three

WHAT WAS HAPPENING? Holy crap, what was happening? Jack Cannon was kissing her.

The Jack Cannon was kissing the ever-loving daylights out of her.

And it was heavenly.

His lips moved with purpose, coaxing her to open and allow the tip of his tongue to sneak inside and delve into her mouth. This was no sloppy version of tonsil hockey, no sir. Jack kissed with the confidence of a man who was aware of his skill. Who knew how to electrify her every sense and make her hungry for more.

When he finally pulled back to gasp for some much-needed air, her vision blurred in and out.

"What is happening?" she slurred.

"I told you. You're smart, you're beautiful. And knowing that for one second you could believe that you are not worthy of affection, well, that's a great injustice."

"So that was a pity kiss?" Ugh. How disappointing.

"No. Hell no. If you let me, I'll show you just how opposite of a pity kiss that was. Darlin', that's just a little morsel."

If that was him giving her a little taste, heaven help her when he delivered the whole cake.

"I'd like to see that," she said, eager for a bite.

"Would you now?" Wicked anticipation curled his lips as he grabbed the hair at the back of her neck and pulled, swooping in to take her mouth with hot open-mouthed kisses.

The bodice of her sundress seemed to constrict around her chest, making it even more difficult to breathe while his other hand caressed her up and down her back, causing heat to erupt over her bare skin. She was on fire all over. Even the skirt covering her legs felt as if she were being smothered by an electric blanket.

She wanted to be closer to him. Needed to be closer. She clutched at his shoulders, digging her fingers into his broad back. Leaning forward, she climbed onto his lap, pushing him against the arm of the couch. The length of his erection pressed against the very heart of her and sent shivers straight to her nipples.

"Does this mean you like me?" she asked with a swivel of her hips.

"Darlin'." He chuckled, desire adding a husky rasp to his voice. "I like you a *lot*. If your brother knew the thoughts going through my head right now, I'd be so dead."

Her brother, right. His boss.

But Mark wasn't *her* boss. Hehehe.

"So I shouldn't do this?" She toyed with the strap of her dress, slowly pulling it down off one shoulder and loving the way his gaze followed.

"Hey, who am I to tell a woman what to do?"

"And what about this?" She pulled the other strap down, revealing a generous amount of cleavage.

Jack stopped her by holding her hands with his. "Before I let this go any further, are you still drunk?"

"Oh, no. I'm sober. This is probably the soberest I have ever been in my life."

"Good. That's good." He smiled and lifted his hand to slowly run the tips of his fingers over the edge of her bodice. He slowly pulled the fabric down, revealing her unbound breasts. "Naughty girl. Running around without a bra."

"When you don't have a lot on top, you take that risk."

He circled the puckered nipple with his fingertip. "You have plenty."

She drew a deep breath and pressed more of her breasts into his hand. He responded by cupping the mound and sucking the tip into his mouth.

Oh, things were escalating quickly. Was she going to do this? Was she really going to engage in some down and dirty sexual activity with Jack Cannon?

The sight of the top of his sandy-colored hair as his teeth worked her nipples, sending tingles throughout her body, made the answer clear.

Hell, yes.

She threw her arms around his head and hugged him against her bosom while she swiveled her hips against his lap in time to her pounding heart.

His hands on her thighs were hot, as if he had been holding them in front of a fire. He slid his palms up her bare thigh and cupped her butt in his hand. She shrieked with surprise as he stood up and carried her across the room.

"Bedroom. Now. If we're gonna do this, I want to do this right."

"Put me down." She wiggled out of his arms. "I'm not going to have you pull something trying to carry me upstairs."

"I appreciate your concern, darlin', but I can handle a little thing like you."

Oh, wasn't he sweet. At 5'10" and a solid size twelve, she

wasn't a wisp of a woman. In fact, she was a little bit taller than him. But hey, let him keep thinking she was dainty.

She had barely hit the light switch when he twirled her around and stripped her dress the rest of the way off her body, dropping the garment to the floor.

"Do you always wear such sexy panties?" he asked, running his rough palms over her lace-covered hips.

"Always."

"Damn, woman. If I would have known…"

"If you would have known…what?"

"I would have indulged in even more naughty fantasies about you than I had been. If your brother knew I thought about you that way, he'd kill me."

"But you're here with me now." She pressed her naked breasts against his cotton-covered chest. "Are you still afraid of him?"

"Darlin', the devil himself could be between us right now and I'd fight him to the death to get to you."

"You're so full of—" He swept her into his arms and kissed her before she could call him on his bullshit.

Jack was one of the best-known flirts in the county. From getting a free slice of pie every time he went to Mindy's Diner, to ending a night at The Crescent Moon Bar with the phone numbers of three different women, the man knew how to work his charm.

Then again, she never saw Jack give those women the look he was giving her. At least not in public. Sparks flashed in those blue irises, and the skin around his mouth tightened as if he couldn't wait to take a bite out of her hide. Heaven help her, she wanted to be his feast.

He pushed her back onto the bed then stripped off his T-shirt before lying down by her side. He cupped her breasts in his hands and buried his face between her cleavage with a small growl.

"These are lovelier than I imagined. So soft." He took one nipple between his lips and tugged. Each lash of his tongue against the tight bud was like a tiny arc of electricity that built into a steady hum.

She couldn't get enough of touching his warm skin, running her hands up and down his back and sides as if she were working a worry stone. Underneath her fingers, the perfection of his golden flesh was marred by the various scars he endured in his lines of work. Barbed wire, rope burns, bull horns, all contributed to the physiology of a cowboy. Tracing the lines, it was as if she was learning his life story by braille, and the tale was both fascinating and frightening.

"I want you completely naked." She tugged at the waistband of his jeans. She didn't want to think about all the close calls he had had in his life. "Please."

"Ah, you say that so sweetly." He stripped her of her panties, then settled her legs over his shoulders with a wicked smile. "But no."

Wait. Was he actually going to go full steam ahead and skip right to the heart of her? Where was the subtle press of his hands on her shoulders for the pre-sex blow job followed by intercourse? If any of her dates had gone down on her, it wasn't until their third time together, at the earliest.

With an eager chuckle, he ran the flat of his tongue between her swollen folds and tickled her clit.

God bless the man, he was.

"Holy hell, Jack," she groaned and dug her fingers into his hair. "That feels so good."

"How bad of a day did you have today?" he asked.

"Terrible."

"All right then." He plunged his fingers into her sheath, rubbing and stroking her inner walls until she gasped and arched into his touch. "That's it, baby girl. You take that."

"Oh my God."

She hung on to his hair as if he were a raft and she was riding the wild rapids down a raging river. In the horizon, the first fall loomed, coming closer with each stroke of his fingers. Did she fling herself off the ledge, or hold on for dear life?

"You're holding back, darlin'. I can feel it. Breathe, sugar. That's it, breathe and let go."

Jack renewed his attention of his tongue on her clit, pitching her over the rapids into the ravine of ecstasy. Dear lord, this is how it must feel to grab onto a 50,000-volt wire. Her heart stopped and her lungs froze as sparks skipped over her body.

"Oh my, Jack. Ah," she moaned and stuttered as the room came into focus.

"That's my girl." He latched onto her wrists and pushed her hands over her head. "Hang on to the edge of the mattress. I like my hair where it is, thank you."

"What?" She blinked as his image continue to blur in and out and she spotted the strands of sandy blond hair between her fingers. "Sorry."

He chuckled. "Don't be. You're about to go again."

"Do what again? Oh!" she gasped and bucked into his touch as his thumb joined in on the assault to her senses.

"You said you had a terrible day. I think three or four more of these is necessary."

He wasn't serious, was he? His tongued delved into her sheath as he glanced up at her with sin and determination in his gaze.

Her body had barely recovered from the first ride down the Jack Cannon Rapids before he plunged her headlong into the next series of dips and falls.

For a second, she considered fighting the currents. Convinced that men didn't care for enjoying a women's essence. But this was Jack. Jack wouldn't mislead her. If he was intent on giving her pleasure, she was going to do her damnedest to relax and give herself up to the tide.

Over and over he brought her to the peak and flung her over the edge as she screamed her pleasure to the rafters. Only when her voice grew hoarse and her limbs felt as substantial as pudding did she weakly tap at the top of his head.

"No more. Please. I can't take anymore."

"You can take it. Come on, Mel. One more."

"Oh." Her body bucked in his hold and the tears streamed down her cheeks as he strummed her inner walls as if she were a guitar, all the while whispering in her ear as if he were the singer.

"You're so sexy, Mel. Do you have any idea how hard you're making me? That's it, squeeze my fingers with that wet pussy."

This was unreal. Who knew Jack was such a dirty talker? And who knew that would make him even hotter?

"Jack. Jack," she panted, feeling the rush of oblivion lap at her conscious. "It's too much."

"Never too much. Come for me, sweet girl." He lowered his head and fixed his lips around her clit and sucked.

A string of unintelligible curse words and grunts spilled from her lips as the wave she rode crashed upon the shore and her body spasmed as if all her bones were about to shatter.

Holy. Shit. From the moment she met him, she knew Jack was sexy. But never did she suspect that he was a sex god of Zeus-level proportions. He was going to kill her with orgasms.

Yeah, and you'll be begging for more with your last breath.

True. So true.

Somehow she found the strength to lift her eyelids to the

vision of a gloriously naked Jack at the foot of her bed.

"Well, hello," she rasped.

The sun had painted his skin in a hodgepodge of patterns that reminded her of a sexy patchwork quilt. The golden tone on his forearms faded into the peach of his biceps and shoulders, and a line marked where the sunlight had kissed the back of his neck. Where his jeans covered his lower body, he was milky-white except where a roadmap of pink lines covered his left thigh down to his knee.

The stories she had heard about his accident were that Jack had almost died of blood loss when a bull had bucked him off then stepped all over him. Seeing those scars and knowing that he was now planning on going back into the arena, although in a different capacity, suddenly didn't seem like a good idea.

"Hi there, yourself," he said, breaking the hold his scars had on her attention. He finished rolling a condom over his thick shaft then crawled over her, settling his slim waist between her thighs. "This is your last chance to tell me no, Mel."

Tell him no? The man just turned her inside out in the most delicious way. Repeatedly. Not only that, he had driven her home and held her hair when she was sick. This was one cowboy she was not kicking out of her bed.

She wrapped her legs around his waist. "Take me, you big stud."

Jack's laugh turned into a snort. "Yes, ma'am."

With the green light to do as he pleased, he surprised her again and held still for several heartbeats. He brushed his finger over her cheek then leaned down and placed a gentle kiss to her lips. The kiss grew hotter like a slow burning flame, quietly consuming her from the mouth down then exploding as he slid the entire length of his shaft into her warm heat.

He pushed up onto his hands and watched her as he thrust

in a steady, languid pace. "You are so sexy."

She smiled in reply and ran her hands over his work-scarred body, kneading his flesh as if he were warm putty, firm yet malleable as she squeezed and stroked his muscled torso.

Having been fully satisfied, she relaxed into the mattress, offering her body for him to take what he needed. She loved the way his muscles flexed and the way his eyes flashed with each plunge. A pink flush raced up his neck, making his cheeks glow.

"Am I boring you?" he asked.

"Not at all. I like watching you."

"Do you?" He swiveled his hips, driving the tip of his cock deep into her core.

"Oh my God. What *is* that?" No one had ever touched her so deep.

"This?" He repeated the movement. "Something I learned from my physical therapist."

"You slept with your physical therapist?"

He bent down and nipped at her breast. "No, silly. This is an exercise that's supposed to relieve stress in my lower lumbar."

"Well, it's relieving *my* stress." Tiny pricks of electricity zipped over her body, and at her center a ball of energy was growing, pulsing with anticipation. "Oh, don't stop."

"A second ago you were begging me stop."

"Jack." She slapped at his chest. "If you stop, I swear to God, I'll scratch your eyes out."

He captured each of her wrists in his hands and trapped them above her head. "As you wish."

The smile that stole across his lips reached his eyes. *I'm gonna fuck you up*, she saw in his expression. *And you're gonna beg me for more.*

Oh, shit. She just spurred the bull, didn't she?

She curled her fingers into fists and braced herself for the ride. Gone was the gentle, rolling tide from the moment before. Not only was she back riding the rapids, this time they were the wildest of the level 5 classes and she was about to fly off Niagara Falls.

"Fuck, Mel." Jack moaned. His nostrils flared, reminding her of one of the beasts he used to try to tame. "I'm gonna come."

Not yet. Please not yet. She was so close, the flames of her release were licking at her cheeks.

"Don't stop," she commanded through gritted teeth. "Don't. Please."

"Mel. Fuck. Melody."

Jack's bellow was lost in the roar filling her ears as her world exploded and she floated in oblivion, cocooned within a cloud of pulsating heat that seemed to go on and on.

The air conditioning unit kicked on, blowing a stream of cold air across her sweat-slickened skin. The chill roused her from the sex-induced coma robbing her thoughts, and she huddled next to Jack's furnace-like body for warmth.

"Damn." He gasped by her side. "Woman. I've never come so hard."

On the tip of her tongue was the urge to make some smartass remark about how he probably said that to all the girls, but she lacked the energy to do more than grunt in reply.

What just happened? What in the hell just happened?

You just had your world rocked, girlfriend.

Duh. That was a given. But her world was rocked by Jack Cannon.

Cold and adrenaline sent tremors racing through her body, making her muscles and limbs twitch as her brain tried to make sense of her reality. Above the chaos, one question swirled in her mind as if she were stuck on a runaway carnival ride.

Now that they had slept together, what happened next?

Chapter Four

"**M**ELODY. I SWEAR. What is with you today?"

"What, huh?" Melody jumped in her seat and rubbed the spot on her arm where her friend and co-worker Erica had slapped her. "What was that for?" she whispered, mindful of the other teachers attending the meeting around them.

"You zoned out. Again. Principal Vincent keeps giving you the side-eye."

She glanced to the front of the room to see her boss watching her with a frown as he continued to go over the latest testing mandates handed out by the state. Flashing him a weak smile, she flipped to the page in the handouts he was discussing and tried to follow along.

"Something's up with you," Erica whispered in her ear. "You and me are going out afterward for wine and talking."

Wine. The devil's brew.

A glass, okay, a bottle of wine was the cause of her current frame of mind, and ever since she had swallowed that evil concoction, nothing had been the same.

Every muscle in her body ached from the restraint she was using to keep from reaching for her phone. Thirty-six hours and twenty-...she glanced on the clock on the wall...seven minutes had passed since her night with Jack, and she had yet to hear a peep from him.

At least he had left a note on her nightstand when he left her house after she had fallen asleep in his arms. Hey, it had been a stressful day topped off with Jack's formidable lovemaking skills. The moment her heartbeat had returned to normal after the second time they had sex, her adrenaline crashed and she had promptly passed out.

"Good morning, darling. Have a good day." He had scrawled in his chicken-scratch handwriting on the back of an envelope and propped it next to a bottle of Advil and a glass of water. She had thought it had been a sweet gesture, until he had gone radio silent.

The lack of communication had been understandable for the first part of the day. With Trey on new-daddy duty and some of the herd being readied for sale, the hands had been extra busy on the ranch. But once the sun had set, and in the Pacific Northwest during the summer that was late in the evening, she had expected a phone call. At the very least a text saying hello.

But nope. Nothing.

Although it galled her on a feminine level, she had taken the big girl/modern woman initiative and made the first move by sending a friendly, yet probing, text.

"Hey. Happy Monday. I'm still sore but in a nice way."

Short, sweet, a little naughty. Sure to elicit some type of a response. Right?

Apparently not. Three hours later, bubkes. And she would know, because she had been sitting on her phone, dying with anticipation for that telltale vibration announcing he finally responded.

And then you'll do what?

Ah, yes. That horrid little question her subconscious kept replaying whenever she thought of her and Jack together, which of course was nonstop.

Then what?

Jack's response could go two ways. Both with life-changing ramifications. If he said he wanted to see her again, what exactly did that mean? Could she picture a future with Jack? One where they went out on dates, fell in love, got married, and had kids?

Yeah, she could. She saw that future real well, which was funny since she hadn't thought about him in that way at all until he laid that kiss on her. A kiss she still felt zipping through her bloodstream.

But oh, could she imagine their future now. Nights spent cuddling on the couch watching movies. Sitting side by side at the bonfires at one of the Armstrongs' cookouts. Camping under the stars as she joined him on the weekends during rodeo season.

If he was going to be a pickup man, he was going to be traveling a few months out of the year. Obviously, if she wanted to be with the man, she was going to have to accept the rodeo, too. Sure, rodeo season wasn't the ideal situation for courting a romance, but it might be exciting to travel all over the Northwest.

She sucked in her lips to keep from grinning like a lovesick fool at the thought of spending each night in his arms. But those were much more pleasant thoughts than the alternative, which she was afraid was the cause of his silence.

If Jack thought that they had made a mistake, or even worse, she was a one-night stand, she'd die, just die. Pity sex because she had been so damn pathetic blubbering over a broken heart and a friend's good fortune would be the ultimate humiliation.

With each passing minute, she grew more fearful that she

had just been a way to pass the time and he didn't want to make things awkward by admitting it. As if seeing each other at least once a week while gathering with their friends and family wasn't going to be awkward enough with their night of passion between them.

Night of passion. She mentally snorted. What, was she in a soap opera or something?

Buzz buzz.

She sucked in a gasp and held still, dying to reach for her phone. It was Jack. It had to be Jack.

Sweat trickled down her hairline despite the air conditioning being cranked to arctic chill, and if forced at gunpoint, there was no way she'd be able to recall a shred of what Principal Vincent said that entire morning.

"Okay, folks," her boss said and looked at his watch.

Please, please, please. Her muscles tensed as she got ready to leap out of her chair.

"That's it for today. We'll reconvene in a month. Please send all your completed course certificates to Mrs. Garcia as you finish. We don't want to burden her all at once as we're preparing for the new school year."

"All right, missy." Erica stood and looped her purse over her shoulder. "Let's go eat. I'm starving and you need to spill your guts. Don't bother to deny it. I can tell."

"There's nothing to tell," Melody said in as carefree a voice as possible and forced her hand to pull her phone from her pockets as if she were merely curious as to what might be displayed on the notifications.

One text message from Jack.

Yes! She swallowed her squeal of delight and shrugged. "I can eat. Are we going to Mindy's or Bittersweet?"

"Bittersweet. I told you, we need wine."

"It's only one p.m."

"Trust me. We'll need wine."

"I'm more in the mood for strawberry lemonade, but you can have all the wine you want. See you there?"

"See you there."

They parted ways and Melody ran the last three feet to her car and climbed inside the sweltering interior. She started the engine and turned the air conditioning to full blast, careful not to touch any part of the vehicle that had been baking in the sun's heat. She held the phone in her cupped hands, staring at it as if it were about to impart some great secret.

She swiped her finger over the screen and opened the message, feeling her heart pound harder with each passing second. What words of loveliness did he send her?

The message opened.

☺

...*What?*

She scrolled forward and backward, looking at the timestamp of the message and searched for any portion that might have come across in separate sections.

That couldn't be it, right? After the night they spent together, the man didn't text her a lone colon and a "close" parenthesis? Did he?

"Son of a bitch." She moaned and curled into a ball around her steering wheel, heedless of the hot plastic burning her through her shirt.

Geez Louise, could she be a bigger dork? Here she'd been, imagining tomorrows and happily ever afters with Jack and apparently he thought their time together was only worthy of a smiley-face emoji.

"What the hell does that even mean?" she shouted to the

powers that be. "Nope. Nope." She shook her head and pinched the bridge of her nose, determined not to cry.

No. No more. No longer was she going to pin her hopes on Mission's "finest," only to be disappointed time and time again. Mission? Ha! More like the entire county was filled with one romantic deadbeat after another.

"I am so done," she muttered and threw the car into reverse, pulling out of the parking lot with the single-minded focus of moving on.

"It's about time," Erica greeted her once she sat in her seat at what they referred to as "their" table at the restaurant. "I was about to jump back in the car and look for you."

"Sorry. Favorite song was on the radio. You know how that is." She slid into the booth and addressed the waiter who was patiently waiting. "Hi. May I have a Moscow Mule, please?"

"Sure thing," he said and went to place their drink order.

"Moscow Mule?" Erica gasped. "What happened to I'll just have a lemonade?"

"I'm turning over a new leaf. I'm tired of the same old, same old. Of brown rolling hills and men in jeans and hats. I'm ready for new."

Erica sighed and rested her cute, pixie-like chin on the back of her hand. "Which fella are we lamenting this week?"

Exactly. That response right there was exactly why her life needed to change.

"I didn't say it was a man. Did I say anything about a man? I just need something new. Something exciting."

"I understand, sweetie." She reached across the table and patted Melody's hand. "So what are you thinking?"

"I'm thinking…" Dare she even go through with it? "I'm thinking…there's a new middle school opening in the city this fall. And three more in the suburbs. They're still hiring."

"Seriously?" Erica gasped. "You'd really leave Mission?"

"Yeah." She glanced at the silent cellphone peeking out of the top of her purse. "I'm ready to go."

JACK STOOD ON Melody's porch and blew out a breath. Raising his hand to press the doorbell, he paused and took a second to catch a whiff under his sweaty arms.

Damn. Why in the hell was he so nervous? This was just his friend Melody he was calling on.

It's because *it's your friend Melody, you jackass.*

Yeah. Right.

Melody. His friend. His boss's sister. His friend's ex-girlfriend. That Melody.

Shit, no wonder it felt as if he was standing at the gate, ready to climb onto the back of the nastiest bull in the show. Sleeping with Melody was either the best thing that ever happened to him or the hugest mistake of his life.

The other night had not been the first time he had thought about kissing Melody Webber. He had meant what he told her when he drove her home. She was beautiful, smart, and way out of his league. Of course he had wondered before what it would be like to kiss her, but as soon as the thought entered his mind he would shut it down.

Then he sat on her couch and held her in his arms. He had known that if he gave in to the urge to taste her lips, he'd cross a line there was no coming back from.

And he crossed the line anyway. Hell, he blew past it and left a trail of flames.

Now he was standing on her porch, uncertain of the welcome he'd receive. Especially since his last text messages had gone unanswered.

He blew out another breath and shook out his hands. *Man up and do it, Cannon.*

The doorbell was hot to the touch from being in direct sunshine. The chime echoed on the other side of the door. He timed the wait for response the same way he did when he sat in the saddle. One thousand one, one thousand two, one thousand three.

When he reached one thousand fifteen, he moved to press the bell again when the door opened.

Melody stood in the doorway, blinking with surprise in the sunlight. She was so sexy in her denim skirt and off the shoulder top in a deep blue. Man, she was a knockout. "Jack. What are you doing here?"

"I, uh. I wanted to see you." Obviously. "I texted you earlier."

"Yeah. I saw that." The sour purse of her lips and the tone of her voice didn't give him the warm fuzzies.

Another bad sign: she didn't open the door all the way, instead peering out at him from the few inches of the opening.

Between Greta, Gabriella, Faith, and more recently Nic, he had been around enough women lately to recognize the signs of a pissed-off female. Something was wrong.

"Can I...come in?"

She sighed. "Why?"

"Melody, what's wrong? Is this about the other night?"

Her eyes widened as she sputtered. "Yeah. You could say that."

Ah, crap. Now she was talking in "women speak." She was pissed. But he still had no clue as to why.

"Let me in. Please. We need to talk."

"Fine," she said with a roll of her eyes. And he thought he heard her mutter, "As if I need more humiliation in my life."

He entered the house, closing the door behind him. He turned around and stopped dead in his tracks. Melody stood at the entrance, her feet braced apart and her arms crossed over her chest, blocking the path to her inner sanctuary.

Jack rubbed his hand over the back of his neck and sighed. "So…I take it you do regret our night together."

Her mouth dropped open and her eyes widened. "Me? *You're* the one who regrets it."

"I do?" He gestured to her defensive body language. "This right here tells me you're not happy."

"You sent me a smiley-face text."

Shit. She was wandering into women talk again.

"Yes. I did," he replied gently, as if he was laying a piece of meat at the foot of a hungry, cornered bear then leaned back, afraid of the repercussion.

Melody flailed her hands like a flag in a windstorm. "How am I supposed to take that?"

"That I had a good time?" What else could he have meant?

"Why didn't you say that?"

"I thought I did."

"No. A smiley-face emoji means 'Whatever, stay away from me, have a nice life.'"

He rubbed the space between his eyes. "Is that why you didn't respond to my other messages?"

Her eyelashes fluttered. "What other messages? The emoji was it."

Ahhh… Understanding was beginning to dawn. "I sent you texts this afternoon. Asking how you were. How your day was. If you wanted to get together tonight."

She reared back. "I didn't get any messages."

"Figures. I was way out in the field when I sent them." He shook his head and dared to reach for her hand. When her fingers curled around his, he sighed. "Melody, I don't regret our night together. Yesterday was crazy at the ranch. And I was with your brother the entire day. I texted you the first chance I had. You know how bad the cell reception is when we're out in the north pasture. I'm sorry if you thought I was ignoring you."

Her eyelashes fluttered again and she chewed on her full lower lip. "Oh. Well. I don't know what to say. I'm really confused. About everything."

"Me too, darlin'." He chuckled. "Can I be honest with you?"

"Yes?"

At least he wasn't the only one confused and uncertain. To see her unsettled boosted his confidence that his instincts about them were correct. "This is new to me. You are not like the other girls I've ever been out with. And our lives are a lot more entwined because I work for your brother. And hell, Trey might as well be your real brother too. I don't want to mess up anything we have as friends. But I like you. I like you a lot. I want to see where this goes between us. If you'll give me a shot?"

Melody licked her lips and shifted her weight from one hip to the other. "You like me?"

He laughed. "I guess I didn't do a good enough job the other night showing you just how much I like you."

She brushed a lock of her dark hair behind her ear and giggled, dropping her gaze as a touch of pink hit her cheeks.

"Can we try this again?" he asked.

"Try what?"

He stepped back outside the house, closing the door behind him, then rang the doorbell. She answered the door with the cutest little frown on her face.

He tipped his hat to her. "Good evening, Miss Melody. Will the prettiest lady in the state like to join me this evening for dinner?"

A smile curled her lips that made the little gold flecks in her eyes sparkle. "Yes. I'd like that very much."

"Then grab your purse, darlin'. No. Actually, wait a second."

He hooked his arm around her waist and hauled her into the curve of his body. Leaning in, he caught her lips in a kiss he'd been thinking about for the last two days. To his delight, she softened in his arms, her lips parting and allowing him to take what he desired.

Melody sighed into his mouth and melted in his arms, her curves molding to his planes. Melody was by far the tallest girl he'd ever been with, but somehow she fit against him perfectly.

She pulled away and blinked at him with sex-sleepy eyes and swollen lips. "I take it by going out we're really just going to go upstairs?"

His hands tightened on her hips. "Tempting, sweetheart. Mighty tempting. But I want to do this right. Let's go into Yakima and do it nice. If the evening goes well, then we'll come back to your place. I'll wine you and dine you," he said, chuckling low and lusty. "Then I'll sixty-nine you."

She rolled her eyes even as she giggled then ran the tip of her tongue along her upper lip. "Promise?"

He put his right hand on his heart and raised his left hand. "On my honor."

"I'm going to hold you to that."

"I hope that's not the only thing you're gonna hold."

The light in her eyes made him consider changing his mind about going out.

"We'll see, cowboy. We'll see."

Chapter Five

"**O**H, NO, MEL. Your French fries broke," Jack said as he snatched a handful of her fries from the basket on her lap and shoved them into his mouth.

"Jack," she groused. "Stop stealing my fries. You know they're my favorite."

"I think it's the fry sauce you like more." He risked losing a hand by swiping one more fry then jumped down from the flatbed of his truck to throw away his trash.

Mmm. She did love Miner's Drive-in's fry sauce. And she bet she'd love it even more spread all over Jack. But he was testing her good will by stealing her beloved fries. She had yet to meet a potato that had done her wrong.

She nibbled on a wedge of crinkle-cut golden goodness and watched Jack as he lifted his cowboy hat off his head and wiped the sweat from his brow with the sleeve of his shirt. She loved watching the cotton stretch over his lean frame. Hell, she loved watching him, period. And now she could openly drool over him and not worry if he caught her staring.

"Man, it's a hot one," he said, guzzling the last half of his soda. "I may need to get another refill."

"That's Central Washington in the summer for you, sweetheart." She munched on another fry and laughed. "At least it's a dry heat."

The few trees that populated the area around Miner's were more for decoration than to offer any shade from the August sun. If they were really concerned about the heat, they could have gone inside the restaurant where it was nice and air conditioned, but both of them enjoyed sitting outside like when the old drive-in had first opened and watch the kids from a visiting school district's marching band play Frisbee in the grass.

"If you go back in, get me more fries." Melody laid back on the foam bedding Adam had set out in his truck for their picnic and settled her sunglasses over her eyes. "And sauce."

"Would my queen care for anything else?" Jack asked with a chuckle.

"A pillow would be awesome."

At that he laughed. "Soon, darlin'. Part of the plans for when I have the Silver Bullet restored is add a chest that can hold all sorts of camping gear. I'll be able to turn the flatbed into a bedroom in no time flat. Sexy, huh?"

Camping wasn't Melody's thing, but with Jack, she'd be willing to give it a try, especially if it meant outdoor sexy times. His imagination when it came to bed sports was one of her favorite traits of his.

"When are you having this work on the truck done? You've been talking about doing it forever."

"Within the year, I hope. I have about thirty-five grand saved up. Just need another five or six more to do it right."

"Wait a second." She popped up to rest on her elbow and looked at him over the rim of her sunglasses. "Dollars? You are sitting on thirty-five *thousand dollars*?"

He nodded with his amiable grin, as if holding on to that much change was commonplace.

"Forty thousand to fix up what my brother calls a 'piece of shit Chevy'?"

"Ouch." He drew back as if she had come at him with a switchblade. He rubbed his palms over the hot metal of the panel of the truck as if soothing an upset child. "Don't listen to her, girl. She's only regurgitating the hate spewed by her ignorant brother. I'll teach her right. Just you wait, Mel. When all the work is done, the Silver Bullet here will be the prettiest thing you've even seen."

"We'll see about that. At least she'll be worth more when she's done."

"Oh, no. She'll only be worth maybe twenty-five when it's done."

Melody's jaw dropped so fast, she thought she heard it pop. "What? Then why are you pouring so much money into her?"

Jack shook his head and chucked her under the chin with his thumb. "It's not about the money. This is the first truck and only truck I have ever bought. Saved for three summers to be able to buy her the moment I turned sixteen. She's taken me all over this country, even given me shelter a time or two when I was low on funds and between rodeos." He got a faraway look in his eyes and his voice turned husky with the memory. "Yep. She's been good to me. And I'll be good to her."

"If you say so." Melody shook her head. "I don't think I'll ever understand boys and cars."

Jack laughed. "That's because you're thinking of boys and cars. I'm a *man*." He slapped the sides of the vehicle. "And this is a *truck*."

"Hey, Cannon."

They both turned toward the sound of the voice. A couple approached them, walking arm in arm and dressed as if they were spending a day at the beach in flip–flops, swimwear, and cover-ups. Since the nearest beach was five hours away, they were probably doing what most people in the valley did on a hot Saturday afternoon and inner tube down the Yakima River.

"Billy. Megan. What up?" Jack said and slapped hands with the tall drink of water sporting a farmer's tan.

"The usual," Billy replied with a snort of laughter. "Where you've been, man?"

"Rock'n and roll'n. You know how it goes. Looks like you're heading to or back from the river."

"A bunch of us are meeting up at the spit. Gonna have a bonfire and make some mischief as always. I know I sent you a text. Hey, Mel."

"Billy." Melody's warm smile for the cowboy turned tight when she focused on his girlfriend. "Megan."

The pretty brunette pixie's smile was just as tight. "Melody."

"Oh, right." Jack stuck his hands in his back pockets and shifted his weight. "Yeah, I have other plans."

"Is it because of my cousin?" Megan asked. "I know you and Stacy had a bad breakup, but I know she'd love to see you. I've heard her say many times that if you would just apologize, she'd take you back."

Melody about choked on her tongue. Stacy was a hosebeast who was not only petty and spiteful, she had attacked Nic and tried to run her off when she started dating Adam. Jack had dodged the pointed end of a bull's horn when he broke up with that type of crazy.

"You can tell your cousin not to hold her breath," Jack said. "And that she'd make better use of her time if she pretended I didn't exist."

"Don't let Stacy keep you away. There'll be lots of smokin'-hot chicks there." Billy sucked in a breath as Megan elbowed him in the side. "Not that I'll be looking. But come out. We'll have a blast."

"Naw, I'm good. Besides, I'm already dating someone new."

"Oh, yeah? Who?" Billy's blue gaze shifted to Melody. "Wait, her? You're dating Melody?"

"Well, actually," Melody started when Jack cut her off.

"Mel? Are you insane? Please. We're just friends."

"Insane"? "Please"? What did he mean by that?

"No, no, I'm dating someone else," Jack continued with a nervous edge in his chuckle. "Someone really awesome. Super hot. And smart. And sexy as hell. It's been going real great."

"And who is this mystery woman?" Megan asked.

"Yeah, who?" Melody parroted with a subtle note in her tone for him to watch what he said next. And why did he have to make it sound as if Melody wasn't good enough for him?

"Ah." Jack ran his hand over the back of his neck. "You don't know her. She's a barrel racer from out in Cle Elum. Met her at the rodeo in Nampa and we connected."

Lame, Cannon. That was so lame. Why didn't he name this fictitious woman "George Glass" while he was at it?

"Anyway…" A red flush that had nothing to do with the summer sun raced up Jack's neck. "You all have fun at the spit. I'll be spending most of my weekends on the road soon working rodeos, but I'll catch you all at The Crescent when I can."

"Sure, Jack. Sure. See ya, buddy." Billy clapped Jack on the back and headed into the restaurant with Megan in tow.

"What the hell was that?" Melody asked. "A barrel racer from Cle Elum?"

"I panicked."

"Why didn't you just tell them the truth? Is claiming me as your girlfriend so bad?"

"What? No. I thought we weren't going to tell anybody about us until we were sure?"

"Sure about what?"

"That we were a thing."

"A thing?"

And here she had been thinking that over the last few weeks they were building a relationship and Jack thought they were working toward being a *thing*. Whatever that meant.

God. What a fool.

"Take me home, Jack." She jumped off the flatbed and stomped to the passenger side of the beat-up Chevy and climbed into the humid interior of the cab.

"Melody. What's the matter?" He joined her in the cab. "Why are you all pissy all of a sudden?"

She closed her eyes and sighed, resting her neck against the seat. "Stop talking and take me home."

Jack allowed her peace for all of the few blocks it took to get them onto the freeway before he tried again.

"I can see you are upset, but I honestly don't know why. If Megan found out we were a couple, it'd be all over Mission as fast as her little fingers can text."

"And you don't want your friends to know we're a couple."

"No." He waggled his finger at her. "I never said that. First, Billy is my friend, Megan is not. Second, I never said I didn't want people to know about us. We agreed to keep it on the down low.

"Because we're only a *thing*," she tried to spat, but the *th*-sound made it difficult.

"Ah-ha," Jack sang. "That's it. All right. Okay, I'm sorry I called what we have a *thing*. I was caught unaware and was winging it."

"It's not that." Mostly. "You made it sound as if having me as your girlfriend was the most ridiculous idea on the planet."

"I did no such thing. The made-up woman I was describing

was you."

Maybe. But that didn't ease the sting when he denied the possibility as quickly as one flicked a bug off their sleeve.

"What?" he asked when she continued to turn her face away. "You want to tell people about us? Okay. Let's head out straight to the ranch and tell your brother."

"No." The word shot out of her mouth like a racehorse from the starting gate.

His eyebrows jumped up and disappeared under his hat. "No? What's wrong? I thought you were ready to tell people."

"Mark is not people. He's Mark."

"You kinda have my nuts in a sling here, Mel. Do you want to tell people or not?"

"Yes. But not Mark. I know," she hastily added when he shot her the side-eye. "Telephone, tell a friend, tell anyone in Mission and word will spread. I just hate that we're hiding."

"You're that afraid of what your brother will think? He hates me that much?"

"He doesn't hate you. And it's not you personally. I don't like talking to him about anyone I date. Especially if it's someone from the ranch."

Jack chuckled. "Yeah. He did give Rafe a pretty hard time when you two were going out."

"I know. And I didn't..." She sucked in the words before she spilled her secrets all over the cab.

"You didn't what?"

"Ah."

Right. Yeah. No way was she going to tell Jack that she was developing feelings for him that could probably be labeled as love. Hell, who was she kidding? She was falling in love with him. Hard.

And there was the crux of her hesitation of telling her brother. Never could she imagine that Jack would hurt her in any way. He was one of the good guys.

But there was that doubt. That teeny-tiny irritation, like when you have your hair cut and a little piece of hair gets caught in the collar of your shirt and scratches the hell out of your skin. Jack was a man and therefore capable of crushing her in ways she never anticipated.

If they continued to keep their relationship secret and they did crash and burn, at least she could pretend that she had dreamt the entire thing to try to minimize the pain of losing him.

But wasn't that setting them up for failure? Preventing her, and him, from treating their relationship as a serious endeavor?

Ugh, it was so confusing.

"I, uh, didn't—I don't want you to have to face the impenetrable stare of Mark Webber," she finally answered.

"I can handle your brother, sweetness."

"Sure," she replied with the barest hint of doubt. Jack probably could take on her brother, but could she?

Jack pulled into her driveway and stopped her before she jumped out of the cab. "Melody, I'm sorry if I made you feel like I'm not happy to be your boyfriend. I am. Really."

Boyfriend? Did she hear that correctly? Did he actually put a label on what he was in relation to her?

A warm and fuzzy sensation raced up and down her back, causing her to curl into a ball on the seat as her face heated. "Well, good. I like being your girlfriend."

That Cannon grin brought out the dimple in his cheek. "I think you more than like it, Melody Webber."

"Don't push it, cowboy."

He reached across the seat and pulled her a few inches closer until she was in his lap with the steering wheel trapping her in place. "I'll tell you what. Next weekend you're at that teachers' retreat and I'm at the rodeo. How about we tell the family after that? Give us a little bit longer to have it just be us?"

"That sounds reasonable."

"Reasonable?" He chuckled. "I'll take that. I'll take this, too."

The temperature in the cab rose to near boiling as Jack laid a kiss on her that made her toes curl in her sandals. She pushed his hat off his head in order to dig her fingers into his overgrown locks and pull his handsome face closer.

"Melody? What the hell?" A pounding on the passenger window followed the exclamation.

Melody wiped away the steam that had collected on the glass and squinted through the smudges. "Jerry?"

"Who's that in there with you?" Jerry hollered.

"Oh my God." Melody climbed out of the truck. "Jerry? What are you doing here?"

"I—uh." His Adam's apple bobbed and a red flush darkened his already ruddy cheeks. "I was coming to see my girl. But instead I see her dry humping Jack Cannon. Mel, how could you?"

"How could I? Wait. What?" She tugged at her hair. "Are you kidding me? Are you freaking *kidding* me?"

"Am I missing something here?" Jack asked, bracing his arms over the hood of his truck after having climbed out.

"Yeah. You're missing the part when you don't mess with another fella's girlfriend," Jerry said and stomped toward Jack with the muscles in his jaw bunched and hands forming into meaty fists.

Beneath his tan, Jack paled for a moment and his eyes widened in terror as the man who was not only a foot taller but a good sixty pounds heavier advanced on him.

"Jerry, stop," Melody shrieked.

Her scream seemed to wake Jack up from his trance. He hauled off and clobbered Jerry right in the kisser with a right hook.

"Don't you think of threatening me or my girl, Galloway," Jack snarled at the farmhand now rolling around in the lawn.

Holy shit. That escalated. This was not good. Not good at all.

"Stop it!" Melody chased after Jack and pulled him back. "Both of you stop. Jerry, I know you came over to break up with me."

Jerry grunted with surprise mid-headshake. "What? I wasn't—"

"Oh please. I know you were, you know how? Because you've broken up with me about a million frickin' times! Good lord, man, you have got to do something about your memory loss. I can't take it anymore."

His face scrunched inward as he climbed to his feet. He winced and rubbed at his jaw. "Memory loss?"

"Yes. You. Fall. Combine. Memory loss." She heard the hysteria rising in her voice, but for the life of her, there was no keeping it in. "Where is your girlfriend Stephanie?"

"Stephanie?"

"Yes. Stephanie. She's your girlfriend now."

"Stephanie?" The lightbulb seemed to click behind his eyes as they widened and his cheeks grew even redder. "Oh yeah, Stephanie. Shoot, Mel. I'm sorry."

"I'm sorry, too. I know it's not your fault." At least she wanted to believe he was to trying to manage his condition and was not purposely being a jerk by having her relive a painful moment of her life. "Can I get you some ice?"

"Naw. I'll be fine. It hurts some, but I can take it."

"Sorry about that, Jerry," Jack said and held out his hand.

"After being jumped, I've developed a knee-jerk reaction if anyone comes at me."

"I understand, I guess." His gaze bounced back and forth at them. "So, you two are hooking up, huh?"

"Yep. We are." Jack hugged her against his side. "This one is a keeper."

Unless you were Jerry, obviously. Which he seemed to sense, because his gaze dropped to the toes of his dusty boots.

"I'll be taking off then. Sorry to have bothered you."

As Jerry shuffled down the drive, Melody wanted to race after him and at least give him a hug. But maybe Jack had literally knocked some sense into him and now he'd remember that their relationship was officially over and had been for some time.

"Well." Jack sighed. "Someone else now knows we are a couple."

"True. But it's Jerry. And he'll probably forget in half an hour. Poor guy."

"I had forgotten you two went out. How many times has he been over to break up with you?"

"At least twenty, if not more."

"Good lord, Mel. I can't tell who I feel worse for right now. No wonder you get all fidgety when it comes to men and relationships."

"I'm not fidgety. Okay," she conceded when he raised his brow. "Maybe a little. As you know, I haven't had the best of luck."

"Their loss, my gain." He pulled her against him and pressed his pelvis into her belly as a wicked grin curled his lips. "And I am so gonna reap what they sowed."

"What does that even mean?"

"It means, Ms. Webber. That I'm gonna take you upstairs."

He dropped a line of kisses up her neck. "Strip you naked. And worship every inch of your luscious body."

She melted against all his manly planes. "Mmmm. That sounds lovely. But how about a quick shower first? I feel sweat collecting in places I didn't even know had a crease."

"No way." He scooped her up in his arms. "Why get clean when I'm just gonna sweat you back up again? I want to revel in your musk."

Ewww. What a way to kill a lady boner. "You've been hanging around the breeding barn too long, haven't you?"

"Darlin', you know the stud doesn't have to do anything but stand there. Oh no, I've got moves the most carnal of creatures have never seen. Soon, I'll have you beggin' for it. Don't you want that, Mel?" His voice lowered and the heat in his eyes intensified, sending sparks over her skin. "Don't you want to be my filthy, dirty, nasty girl?"

She did. Heaven help her, when he looked at her with heat simmering in his blue eyes, she wanted to spread her thighs and yell at him to come and get her.

"Yes, please," she whispered.

"Good girl." He chuckled, low and husky.

Lady boner back on.

Chapter Six

"E ASY, GIRL. EASY." Jack ran his palm down the long
length of his mare's neck. "Don't let those cows get
the best of you."

If he were to be honest, the words were more for him than
for Roxanne. Appaloosas didn't take shit from anyone, and were
the perfect horse for him to drive pickup. As his training
advanced, he'd bring a second horse as backup, but Roxanne
would always be his main gal.

It had been three years since he had last been inside an arena. Two years since he could look at anything having to do with
the rodeo. Man, did he miss it.

Closing his eyes, he reconciled the memories of the past and
the reality of his present. The sun beat on his back, and in the air
was the scent of prime rib sandwiches mixed with popcorn, cow
manure, and cotton candy. In his mind, it wasn't his horse
beneath him but a two-thousand-pound Angus named the Mad
Hatter. The muscles in his legs spasmed as he also remembered
all two thousand of those pounds crashing down on him and
destroying his dreams.

Instead of returning home to Pendleton as a rodeo champ,
he returned broken. Uncertain if he ever would, or even wanted,

to get back in the ring.

Now here he was. Not quite back to living the dream, but still back to where the action was. Back with the people, back with the animals, back experiencing the excitement of another rodeo and the challenge of man conquering beast.

"Holy shit. Jack? Is that you?"

Jack jumped down from the saddle and reached out to shake the man's hand, pumping his arm as if he was searching for water. "Sterling. Hey, man, good to see you."

Sterling resettled his bull rope over his shoulder and pushed the brim of his hat out of his eyes. A few more scars cut across his cheek, but he wore the same lopsided grin that wooed many a girl when they ran the circuit together.

"What are you doing here?" He gestured to Roxanne. "Are you roping now?"

"Nope." Jack tied his horse to a fence then settled his hands on his hips. "I'm training to ride pickup."

Sterling removed his cowboy hat and ran his sleeve over his sweaty brow. "No shit? That's awesome. Where the hell have you been the last three years?"

Together they walked toward the competitors' dressing room while Jack did a quick play-by-play of his time spent at the Sprawling A.

That first step across the threshold to the dressing room was as if he had jumped through a portal in time. The *chink* of buckles, reins, and spurs melded with the manly murmurs of conversation that ranged between preseason football to women.

Most of the faces were new, and to his chagrin, baby-faced. Damn, had they even graduated high school yet? Did he ever look that green?

Jack took a seat on a bench while Sterling arranged his gear. "You're doing well in the rankings this year. Climbed a few places since Lynden."

Sterling shrugged. "Not where I'd like to be, but I'll end up with a profit this year." A slow grin broke across his face. "Jen and me are having a baby."

"Jen? As in that cute little redhead you met in, where was that, Boise?"

"No, that was Jenna Tompkins. I married Jen Jorgensen. She was the shot girl at the rodeo in Boulder."

"Right. Blond Jen. Wow. That's amazing. Congratulations, man."

A few more men entered the room and one of them stopped and clapped with glee. "Well, shoot. Lock up your daughters, 'cause Cannon and Atkinson are together again."

"Hey, Bucky." Jack stood and shook the hand of the older gentleman who was going to be his trainer for the next few rodeos. "Good to see you again."

Bucky laughed and slapped Jack on the back with his free hand. "Good to see you, old boy. Glad to have you back in the show."

"Wait." A fresh-faced lad of about eighteen looked up from packing his cheek with a wad of chew. "Are you Jack Cannon?"

"Maybe. Does he owe you money?"

"No, sir."

"Sir"? Jack winced. Damn, he wasn't even thirty yet.

"Is it true," the kid was saying, "that at the Omak Rodeo, you pulled your ACL getting it on with the entire rodeo court but was able to continue and ended up winning?"

"The rumors that get passed along." Jack shook his head. "What's your name, kid?"

"Cody. Cody Haynes."

"Sorry to burst your bubble, but that's not entirely true."

"Yeah," Sterling piped up. "It was only two of the princesses and he pulled a hamstring."

"But I did go on to win," Jack finished with a grin.

"Wow. Man. You're my hero." The kid had stars in his eyes.

"Hey, Jack." Sterling slapped him on the arm. "Remember the time we went skinny dipping in the river with those cocktail waitresses in Reno and got sunburned all over? Made riding that afternoon real interesting."

Interesting, hell. He almost missed the rodeo, his sunburn was so bad. Fortunately, he and Sterling looked so similar in height, build, and coloring, they had traded places so Jack could take the later draw and hope that the pain medication kicked in before his time in the chute. A risky move since if they had been discovered, they both could have lost their permits. But if Jack hadn't competed, there'd have been no way he could've afforded the repairs on his truck. And without his truck to get to the next rodeo, his year would've been over.

Sterling knew Jack's year had been on the line and agreed to what was probably a stupid plan to start with, but fortune had smiled upon them, and their gamble had paid off. Beneath their helmets and riding gear, no one realized they had switched places.

With new ears to listen to their stories, some of the older cowboys began to regale the young bucks with tales from rodeos past. Each story was raunchier than the next, and Jack's sides began to ache from laughing so hard. He couldn't wait until later that night to tell Melody all about it when he spoke to her on the phone.

"Sounds like you're having quite the ball," Melody said. Her laughter through the speaker made the phone vibrate against his ear. "Part of me wishes I was there to hear all about your young-stud antics, but the other part of me thinks I'm better off not knowing."

"Ha-ha. Maybe. The only thing to make this weekend perfect is if you were here beside me." He rolled over on his makeshift cot on the flatbed of his truck and hugged his pillow. To save money, it was either sleep in a tent on the flatbed or share the trailer with Roxanne. He loved his horse, but not that much.

Melody's sigh was filled with such longing, he could feel it across the distance. "Wish I was with you, too. Thank you for sharing your pictures of the rodeo."

"And thank you for sharing pictures of your magnificent cleavage." Yeah, he was getting better at the whole texting thing and making sure he was sending her more than just an emoji. "You are welcome to send me photos of more than just your boobs, you know. Although I am rather fond of your boobs."

She giggled like a vixen, sending bolts of arousal through his body. "I would if I could." She lowered her voice. "But I don't think my roommate would care to see me take naked pictures of myself."

"Have you asked? I bet she'd even take them for you."

"Ha-ha, Cannon. You're hysterical," she said with heavy sarcasm.

"Where are you, anyway? I hear a funny echo."

"I'm in the stairwell of the motel they have us at for this retreat. I didn't want to be overheard."

"Does that mean you're going to say scandalous things to me?"

"Do you want me to?"

"Oh baby, I do. You know I do." He rolled onto his back and slipped his hand down the front of his jeans. During their recent time together, he learned that his girl had quite the sexy imagination with a mouth to match.

His girl. Yeah, Melody was his girl. And as she spun tales about all the wicked, naughty things she wanted to do to him when he returned, for the first time in his life, he cursed having to work the rodeo.

"Oh, did I tell you I won a gift certificate to Victoria's Secret?" she asked.

"No you didn't. Good job, sweetheart."

"Yep. I wonder what I should get…lacy bra? Satin panties? Would you like that, Jack? Seeing me in frilly lingerie?"

"Darlin', I love seeing you in anything. But especially the frilly girl stuff."

The husky notes in her giggle went right from the phone down his spine to the aching shaft in his hand. Damn, he wished it was her hand working him over.

"Hey, Cannon." Several male voices whooped, and suddenly his truck began to rock from side to side.

"Jack?" Melody asked. "What's going on?"

Sterling's head popped through the opening of the tent. His huge smile flashed in the shadows. "You didn't think we were gonna let you turn in early, did you, Cannon?"

"It's eleven at night."

"Exactly. The party's just getting started."

"But I'm talking to my girl, man."

"Ah. That explains the chub. Put your dick away, say good night to the girl, and let's get to it."

"But—"

Jack knew his protests were lost causes as the rocking of his truck renewed with a battle cry and Sterling tried to grasp his feet and drag him through the opening. Jesus. How many guys were out there, anyway?

"Go," Melody said. "Call me tomorrow."

"Are you sure, darlin'?"

"No. But I know those are your boys. They're excited to see you. Just don't get arrested or wake up next to another woman."

"Never, sweetheart. Love—" Damn. He bit his lip with indecision.

Was it too early to say the "l" word yet? Probably. But damn, it felt so right, so natural.

Hmmm…if anything, he could at least wait until he could tell her in person. His scruffy mug to her beautiful face.

"Love chatting with you, darlin'," he finished and rolled his eyes at his own lameness. "Talk to you soon."

"Good night, Jack." She finished with a series of kissing noises he copied.

"Ah," Sterling cooed. "That's so sweet. Now, let's party."

"All right, all right. This one night only. Tomorrow, I'm talking to my girl."

Sterling shook his head and adjusted the angle of his hat. "Never thought I'd see the day when Jack Cannon went all in on a girl."

"Funny. I thought the same thing about you." Jack jerked on his boots then jumped down from the flatbed. "What? You don't call Jen each night?"

"Of course I do. I just do it earlier in the day and keep it short and sweet. That way I have something to talk about when I get home. A little attention to the wife, leaving plenty of time for shenanigans. It's all about having your cake and eating it too."

The other men around them mumbled and nodded.

Jack laughed and slapped Sterling on the back. "Lord almighty, I'd forgotten how dumb we are. Okay, boys. Let's do this."

Yeehaw!

THE ANNOYANCE OF being away from his girl faded in the morning sun as he worked with Bucky and the other pickup man, Steve, to learn the finer points of their job. These men were the unsung heroes of the rodeo. These were the men who watched out for danger and put themselves between an athlete and an angry bronco. They roped in the wayward calf and corralled the animals to keep the competitors safe. It was hard work, and Jack realized he had taken for granted the men who did their best to protect him.

By midday on the last day of the rodeo, Jack ached in places he hadn't felt in years. It was a different set of muscles they used when rodeoing than during ranching. Both jobs were good, honest work, but he hadn't worn such a huge smile on his face since he started spending time with Melody.

Jack approached the warm-up area where competitors could stretch, lift weights, and jump on any of the apparatuses used to work out last-minute kinks in their form. It was the time of day where those who still had a shot at the grand prize prepared for the day's events and those who had given up hope or were injured were sleeping off the night's drinking and whoring around.

Yep. It was the perfect time of day for him to maybe, just maybe, find a second to jump on top of a bucking barrel and relive a few minutes of his glory days.

But the fates didn't have that opportunity in store for him, as Sterling was already on the apparatus. The cowboy was slowly rolling his hips, adjusting left and right as the stock contractor, Clay Thurston, heckled from the side.

"Don't know, son." The fringe of Clay's silver mustache twitched with his smirk. "Stampede comes from some of the finest buck stock there is. You gonna have to try harder than that."

"We'll see about that, old-timer. I'll cover your bull and get the best score to boot." Sterling laughed.

"I'd watch yourself, Sterling," Jack said and walked deeper into the room. "Clay here supplied the bull that took me out three years ago."

"Are you doubting my skills, brother? I thought we were friends." His frown was evident even through the mask on his helmet.

"Not at all," Jack replied. "I'm hoping that you stick it to the man and put his bull down good."

Sterling let out a huge laugh as Clay waved him off with his big hands. "Sour grapes, Cannon. Sour grapes."

Talking smack with Clay had always been a highlight of Jack's rodeo experience. Clay not only bred some of the finest bucking stock in the circuit, he was always available to coach the riders in the best way to ride his stock to make both his animals and the cowboy look good.

"Good luck to you, Sterling," Jack said and turned to leave the cowboy to his training. The *clip-clop* rhythm of the dulled rowel of Sterling's spurs hitting the leather-covered barrel followed him to the exit.

"That's it, son," Clay was saying. "Give 'em a good show and you'll score both of us loads of points."

"I got it. I got—ah!" Sterling bellowed. "Fuck."

Jack turned and saw an empty bareback barrel with a jean-clad leg hung over the top. Sterling lay beneath the contraption on the sawdust-covered ground, rolling on his side while holding his arm to his chest.

"Shit. Shit, shit, shit," he groaned.

Jack raced over and fell to his knees to hover over him with Clay by their side. "What happened?"

"Don't know," Clay replied for a moaning Sterling. "One minute he pulled back, next minute he was on the ground."

"Shoulder," Sterling groaned. "Torqued it somehow. I can't

feel my arm."

"Well it sure looks like you're feeling something," Jack said, nausea filling his belly as flashes of injuries past flitted through his mind. Remembering that tide of fear that this time the injury was going to be too much for the body to bear and there wasn't any quick fix the sports medicine team could provide that was going to put you back on the animal.

"Let's get you to the doc." Jack slid his arm underneath Sterling's good shoulder.

"No." Sterling shook his head. "Get me to my camper."

Together, Jack and Clay helped Sterling to stand and escorted him toward the parking lot where the cowboy had set up camp for the weekend.

"I can walk," Sterling said, shrugging off their hold with a grimace. "Let's not draw attention."

Jack pasted a fake smile on his lips as they passed some of the other competitors on the way to Sterling's camper on the other side of the arena. As they neared, Clay ran ahead and opened the door. Jack steadied Sterling up the stairs with his hand braced behind his back.

"Boy, that shoulder looks like it popped out of the socket," Clay observed.

"Feels like it, too." He tried to rotate his shoulder and cursed, collapsing on the small bed. "Help me get this damn helmet off."

Jack worked the strap, and together they removed the helmet off Sterling's sweaty head. Not only was the cowboy drenched, but his color was as white as milk and his lips were drawn in a tight line.

Sterling bent over and ripped off his riding glove with his teeth. "Dammit. I can't even make a fist."

"You know you can't compete with that arm," Jack said. "At

least not today. You have nothing to grip with."

"I gotta. I gotta break the top six to have a go at the finals." Hopelessness filled his eyes. "I need that prize money for the new baby."

"And I need a rider for my bull," Clay added. "With a good showing here, Stampede can make it to the PBR. And I need that contract to keep the ranch going."

"The doc is gonna to take one look at your face and ground you. There is no way you're riding today." Jack shook his head. No one understood better than he did the hit to the pride that came with withdrawing from a rodeo, but Sterling was in danger of sustaining a career-ending injury if he continued. "Sorry, Clay. You have to find another rider for that bull. Better luck next week."

Clay rubbed his hand over his face, across his jaw and behind his neck. In the man's eyes, Jack could see him watch revenue from having a bull in the Professional Bull Riders circuit fly away. "There's gotta be a way. There's gotta."

With surprising strength, Sterling reached out and latched onto Jack's shirtfront with his good arm. "I know of another rider. You."

"Me?" Jack pointed to his chest. "What do you mean, *me*?"

"Reno. When we switched places. We can do it again."

"Are you insane? Let's ignore the fact that it would be breaking a major rule, I haven't ridden in three years. I don't have any equipment."

Clay clapped his hands and rubbed his palms together with glee. "Shoot, son, it's like riding a bike. And you're a great rider, Jack. You can do it. It's only eight seconds."

Only eight seconds.

On the back of a bull, eight seconds is forever.

"You're just as insane as Sterling, old man."

"Jack, please." Sterling's grip on his shirt tightened. "I just need top six."

"Top six." Jack's chuckle bordered on the hysterical. "Sure. No problem."

"Think about it, Jack." Clay's mustache quivered. "Haven't you ever thought about riding again?"

Every damn day.

Dreaming was one thing. Doing, another. One didn't just jump onto the back of a bull. There was training, strategy, routine.

But to ride again. To feel that rush of adrenaline burning in his veins, the flex of the beast beneath him as they tried to knock him off. Man versus animal. A fight for dominance. Then the thrill of landing on your feet, or your knee if you're doing it right, or your side and occasionally your head, but jumping off that animal knowing that for a moment in time you were king. To feel that again…

"I'll…I'll do it," Jack heard himself say.

What did you just do?

I don't know. I think I agreed to ride a bull.

You dumb fuck.

Maybe.

While his brain struggled to believe the words that had just come out of his mouth, Clay clapped with glee and Sterling wilted with a sigh of relief. "Thank you, Jack. Thank you."

"Yeah, well, you can thank me afterward. When I'm in one piece."

The knock at the trailer door made them all jump. "Atkinson, are you in there? Thirty minutes till start," the voice called from the other side.

"I'm coming," Sterling hollered.

"We don't have much time," Clay whispered and searched

the room. "Let's get Jack some gear."

Jack helped Sterling out of his chaps and changed them out for his own. Then he slipped the protective vest over his shoulders. Clay handed him a riding glove and the bull rope.

Yep. He was insane. It was going to be hard enough riding with little preparation, and damn near suicidal in borrowed equipment.

So why was he salivating with anticipation?

"Do you have a spare mouth guard?" Jack asked, not ready to delve into the reasons why he was willing to take such a risk.

"In the bag with the rest of my equipment," Sterling replied.

Jack tied the end of the bull rope to the faucet of the tiny sink and began to prepare the rope with rosin. He'd preferred it to do it at the stalls, but he didn't want to risk being in the public eye for longer than necessary.

Clay handed him a helmet and together they left for the arena. With each step toward the stadium, Jack felt the thumping and applauding of the crowd rise through his feet and up his chest.

"Atkinson," one of the flankmen shouted. "About damn time you got here. There are two ahead of you."

"Over here, son." Clay tugged on his arm. "Stall three. Right here."

"Good luck to you, Sterling," some of the other competitors called out as Jack neared.

Jack gave a wave and a small nod but his gaze was focused on the bull rocking his weight back and forth in his chute.

Muscle memory guided his movements as he tied his bull rope to the gate and rolled through a few quick warmups. There was a signal and before he realized it, he was climbing over the gate and settling himself over the back of the beast.

Stampede shuddered and shook, knocking Jack's knees into

the metal stall.

That's right, you big piece of beef. Work out some of that energy.

The spotter laid a hand on Jack's shoulder. "Anytime, Sterling."

Jack's world narrowed down to the tan hide of the beast beneath him, the weathered glove surrounding his hand, and the frayed rope sticky with rosin encompassing the bull.

He let his mind go blank and released three quick breaths out through his nose. Before he thought twice, he lifted his left hand and gave the nod. The gate opened and the bull shot out in a bid for freedom.

The roar of the crowd faded until Jack heard only the pounding of his heart. His vision faded while the clock counted down in his head.

One thousand one.

Back and forth the bull whipped him around as if Jack was something sticky stuck to the end of his finger.

One thousand two.

Holy shit, am I really doing this?

One thousand three.

Stampede swung to the left then to the right.

One thousand four.

Shit. Keep it together. Your arm will not be ripped off.

One thousand five.

Stampede went into a spin and faded, slowly gaining momentum.

One thousand six.

You got this, you son of a bitch.

One thousand seven.

Almost there.

One thousand eight.

That's right, you rat bastard, I got you this time.

Jack paused for the space of a breath for extra measure, then let go of the rope and jumped for dear life. He hit the dirt and rolled, finishing on his knees.

He shook his head to clear his vision and searched for the clock. There it was, right there. Eight seconds. A full ride.

Yeah. Fuck, yeah. He pounded the ground with his fist. He fucking did it!

"Way to go, Sterling," came the cheers from behind the chutes.

Sterling? Oh, right. Sterling. He was supposed to be Sterling, who was now injured.

On shaky knees, Jack wobbled to stand and held his arm to his side, playing up that there might be something wrong with his limb. With his free hand, he gave a wave to the crowd and bolted for the exit.

It was a gauntlet of men and animals as Jack tried to make his way out of the arena without having to stop and talk to anyone. Fortunately, most of the focus was on the next rider and he could ease past with a simple nod or handshake.

Clay met him outside the arena. "You did it, boy. I can't believe it. Holy shit." He finished his praise with a good solid whack on Jack's back.

"Thanks, Clay. But I'm supposed to be injured, remember?"

"Right. Sorry."

One of the physical therapists ran up and waved him down. She gestured to the sports medicine trailer. "You seem to be favoring your shoulder. Let's take you inside and get a look at that."

"It's fine. I got it," Jack slurred around his mouthpiece. He followed up with a few nods and shook off the medic. "I'm good."

"Don't worry, Doc," Clay said. "I'll help him get his gear off and bring him to you right quick."

Jack and Clay scurried to Sterling's trailer before another bystander tried to stop them.

The second he made it inside, he ripped off the helmet and spat out the mouth guard.

"Holy shit. Can't believe I did it," he panted, resting his hands on his knees.

"You did?" Sterling exclaimed from where he rested on the miniscule bed. "It worked? You covered?"

"He sure did," Clay replied. "Scored an eighty-two."

"Eighty-two?" Sterling slapped his thigh with his good hand. "That did it. That got me into the finals."

Jack nodded, only half listening to their exclamations. Possibilities he hadn't dared given hope to made excitement crawl through his belly.

He did it. Not only had he covered the bull, he scored well, too. Sure, his body felt as if he'd run through a cycle in the dryer with a bag of rocks, but his thighs twitched with only the strain of a good workout. His back was sore as hell, but nothing that a good massage couldn't take care of.

"Thank you, Jack. Thank you." Sterling settled back with a relieved smile on his lips. "Las Vegas is one step closer."

Jack allowed Sterling to have his moment. Why tell the man when he was down that he was just about to get a new competitor standing in his way to the championship?

Jack Cannon was back.

Chapter Seven

MELODY PLACED ONE hand on her sternum and the other on her belly. She swore that at any moment her insides were going to burst from her skin and run screaming out the door. She alternated between pacing the length of her living room and sitting in the chair by the front window to peer through the blinds, waiting on Jack's arrival. He wasn't due for another fifteen minutes, but her anxiety would not allow her sit still.

The news she received that morning meant her life was going be a little different. Hell, erratically different. And before her lay several paths, with each fork of the journey more intimidating than the next. As she ran the different options over and over in her mind, she knew that no matter what direction she chose, she wanted Jack to be a part of her future.

She hoped he might want that as well, but it was too much change too soon, and the coin could land in any direction. Until she saw his face, watched to see if he smiled or frowned as she made her announcement, could she be certain of his feelings. It was that fear of his reaction that made her go to the window again and again as she strained to hear his truck pulling up her driveway.

"Oh, thank God," she sighed when she saw the beat-up front end of his truck coming down the street and park in her drive.

Damn. He was so cute in his tight blue jeans and the amber and light-yellow plaid shirt covering his muscular chest. The top few buttons were left open, displaying his golden chest to perfection.

Only the brilliance of his smile and the light in his eyes had the power to take her attention away from his glorious muscles. There was a palpable excitement radiating off him she could sense from twenty feet away as he strode up the walk. He looked so happy. A picture of happiness personified. At the end of the evening, she hoped he still retained that level of joy.

It took everything within her not to rush to the door and fling it open when the doorbell rang. Instead, she took a breath and counted slowly to ten before opening the door.

"Jack. You're early. How nice," she said with her best surprised expression.

"Hey, beautiful." He stepped across the threshold and pulled her into his arms, crushing the bouquet of tulips he held in his hands against her back as he swung her around. "I missed you."

The room continued to spin as he set her down. Oh, that wasn't good. She tried to cover her dizziness with a smile. "I've missed you too. So. I take it the last day of the rodeo went well?"

"Did it ever. I have so much to tell you."

"Funny. I have a lot to tell you too." Boy, did she ever.

"First, these are for you." He handed her the slightly smooshed bouquet before he took her back into his arms and brushed back the strands of hair clinging to her cheeks. "And second…"

Huh. Funny how a kiss could soothe yet distract all at the same time.

Over the last month, she had thought she had become a connoisseur of Jack's kisses. Her absolute favorite was when she drove him to the brink of mindlessness and he was ready to toss her onto any flat surface and have his wicked way with her. But her second favorite were his hello kisses. Those kisses were hot and soft. They seem to say *Hello, I missed you, and I'm so glad to be with you* without making a sound.

When she could no longer breathe, he pulled away and trailed butterfly-soft kisses against her cheek with a final one pressed against her nose before he laid his forehead against hers.

"Damn, woman. You always make me forget what I was about to say."

"I feel the same way." She forced herself to step away from the comfort of his arms and tugged on his hand for him to follow her into the kitchen. "Let me get these flowers into some water and we can talk. Tell me about your weekend."

"It was awesome. You know, it wasn't until I was there, sitting on top of Roxanne, hearing the crowds cheer and having that scent of earth, cow, and corndogs filling my nose, that I realized just how much I missed being part of the show. You have no idea how glad I am that you'll be with me there this coming weekend." A sly smile stole across his lips. "But the weekend's not gonna go quite like we planned."

She paused with the blades of the scissors at the end of the tulip stems. "What do you mean?"

"Do you remember I told you about seeing my friend Sterling again? The one I competed with?"

"Yes."

He rubbed his hand over the back of his neck. "Well, he had a bit of an injury and couldn't finish his last ride."

When he paused and fidgeted with the brim of his hat, a queasy sensation began in her belly. "Is he okay?"

"What?" Jack blinked as if surprised by her question. "Oh, yeah. Dislocated his shoulder, but he'll be fine."

"That's good," she replied, but for some reason her unease didn't fade. In fact, it grew to encompass her body and caused her hands to tremble.

"Yeah…" He rubbed his jaw. "As I was saying, he couldn't finish his last ride, so I, I—I stepped in."

"Stepped in? I don't understand."

His smile widened. "The stock contractor needed the bull to have a good showing. Sterling couldn't ride, so I took his place."

"Took his place? As in you rode a bull?" Flowers forgotten, she dropped them on the counter and rushed to his side, running her hands over his chest and shoulders. "Are you okay? Did you get hurt anywhere?"

Jack laughed. "I'm as right as rain, darlin'. A few bruises and some body aches, but nothing a little bit of working out won't take care of. But I rode, Mel. Hell, I didn't just ride. I covered and scored in the 80s."

"That's great?" The roiling in her belly continued as if warning her there was more to come.

"That's fantastic! So that's what I meant by this weekend will be a bit different than planned." He retrieved a piece of paper from his back pocket. Unfolding the paper with a flourish, he slapped it on the counter. "Instead of being a pickup man, I'm entered."

He entered.

He entered?

"I don't think I understand," she mumbled. And she wasn't certain if she wanted to.

"I entered." He tapped his finger on the paper. "I'm gonna ride bulls again."

"You mean forever?" she practically screeched.

"Well, for as long as I can." He chuckled. "At least through the season. Beyond that would depend on how my body takes the stress. But I hope I have at least another two to three years in me."

"Well that's, that's something." She tried to muster an ounce of excitement, but for the life of her, she just couldn't find the energy. This was not in her future plans at all.

Jack stood there with his arms held out for an embrace with that huge smile on his face and her heart sank.

How could she deny the absolute joy he was clearly feeling for rediscovering his love for the sport he had thought he could no longer participate in? But in her head the memories of the scars crisscrossing his legs like the lines on a road map seemed to grow and lengthen. What if he was injured again? What if this time instead of a slight limp, he couldn't walk at all, or worse?

The excitement slowly started to die in Jack's eyes and his smile faltered. "What's the matter? Aren't you happy for me?"

"Yes. Yes, I'm happy for you." She forced the words she knew he wanted to hear past her frozen lips. "As long as the doctor says you're healthy enough to compete."

"Sure, sure. The doc gave me the all clear today. Right after I got the word, I went and signed up for this weekend's show. This late in the game I'd usually have to be on standby, but they made an exception for me." He winked.

"Well. I guess that's it, then? I wish you well," she stuttered, running her hands down her jean-clad thighs and trying to focus on something, anything, other than the possibility of Jack lying broken on the arena floor.

Stop it. Stop it, she told her overactive imagination. Jack was a professional. *He knows what he's doing. Right?*

Right?

Her gaze landed on the discarded tulips and she went back

to her work, attacking the stems with all the concentration as if she were performing major surgery.

For how long she remained quiet, ignoring the proverbial bull in the room, she didn't know. But it was long enough that when Jack placed his hands on her shoulders, she jumped with a startled shriek.

"You're not happy," Jack said with a tinge of disappointment in his voice.

Damn.

She sighed and bit her lip. "Well, it's not that I'm not happy. I'm just worried. About you and your safety."

He pressed his cheek against hers and hugged her tight around the waist from behind. "I understand that, I do. But, Mel. It was so good to be back in the game. To have that feeling that my heart is about to jump out of my throat. It was awesome."

She patted his hands that he rested on her belly. Anxiety filled her throat, restricting her vocal chords and shortening her breath.

"Hey." He pulled back and turned her to face him. "You said you had some news, too. What's going on?"

A near-hysterical giggle burst forth. "Yeah. Well, I have some news."

"Let's hear it, darlin'."

"Well." Geez, at this point she had said the word "well" so many times, she could've dug her own in the backyard and retrieved a bucket of water already.

She stole a few extra moments to gather her thoughts by rinsing her hands then drying every droplet of water from her skin with the kitchen towel before she placed the cloth on the counter and turned to face him. "I guess I'll start at the beginning. This morning I heard back from the school district I had sent an application to."

"Wait, wait, wait." He made the gesture for a time-out. "School district?"

Melody flicked her hand as if what she had said was no big deal. Besides, she had bigger issues to deal with. "Just one of the school districts near the city. I applied for one of the teaching positions about a month ago."

"Whoa, girl. This is all new to me. You want to move away?" A frown pulled at his lips as if she had taken away his favorite pair of cowboy boots. "I didn't know you wanted to leave Mission."

"When I applied I was considering it. I mean, there was really nothing here for me to stay for." If only he hadn't sent that damn smiley-face text. "And I wanted to try something new. So I sent in an application. Apparently they liked what they saw because they called me today for an interview."

"Wow, Mel. That is some news." He rocked back on his heels and rubbed his hand over his sternum.

"I mean, the position sounds great. More money, better benefits, smaller class sizes."

Rambling. You're rambling. Just spill it.

"So when are you going for your interview?" he asked, shoulders slumping as he stuck his hands in his pockets.

"They wanted me to come in next week." She licked her lips. "But I told them no."

Surprise flashed in his eyes. "No? You said no?" He let out a relieved laugh. "You said no. That's a good thing, right?"

"Well." She winced. "I...I guess so. The reason I said no was partly because of us. I like the idea of you and me together."

"I like the idea of us together, too." He flashed her a wink.

"Ha-ha," she chuckled with both nerves and hope. "But I also said no because...because I'm pregnant."

Jack's eyelashes fluttered, and his face lost all expression except for his eyes. It was as if she could see through the blue iris to the parts of his brain that were working on clicking together and comprehending her words.

"You're...pregnant."

"Yes."

More seconds passed with nothing but the sound of her heartbeat filling her ears.

Finally, his gaze shifted to the left then right as he slowly backed up until his legs hit a dining room chair and he fell on his backside onto the seat with a whoosh of breath. "You're pregnant."

She pinched her lips together and nodded.

His gaze searched the room again for several moments until he looked at her and asked, "Are you sure it's mine?"

Wait. What? *What?*

If it was possible to do a spit take with an empty mouth, she would have done so at that very moment.

Of all the ways she imagined Jack responding, that was not one of them. The mere fact that he doubted the parentage of her baby hit her like a kick in the head from a mare.

"Is it yours?" she sputtered as the words caught in her throat "Is it yours?"

The top of her head felt as if she was going to blow like a volcano.

She didn't even know what to do with that question. *How dare he?*

With her brain turning into a ball of heated rage, she flew to where he sat and slapped at his arms and shouted, "Out. Get out. Get out. Get out. Get out."

"I'm sorry," he said and stood, grabbing her by the wrists. "I'm sorry. That was a jackass thing to say. You just caught me off guard."

"You and me both, bub. But that doesn't give you the right to be an asshole."

"I'm sorry. Really, Mel. I'm sorry." He held her wrists and waited until her breathing evened out. "I'm trying to understand. I thought you were on the pill."

"I am." She pulled away. "Believe me, I've been thinking about that. If I do the math, that was the week we first hooked up. I had that bad cold and was taking medication. It probably made my pills ineffective. But you had condoms. How long had you kept that thing in your wallet?"

That's right, bub. Don't go pinning this all on me.

"Not that old. Stacy bought them just before we broke up..." Suddenly, his posture straightened, and he gazed off into the distance as if trying to remember.

"Hold the phone. You used condoms with me that your ex-girlfriend gave you?"

"Hey. A condom is a condom. And it wasn't as if I had planned on sleeping with you and I thought ahead to get new ones," he replied. "But I do wonder. I had thought it was because you seemed extra excited."

"What do you mean?"

He rubbed his hand over his jaw. "Not to get too graphic, I remember the condom being extra wet. I thought that was hot because we had both been really turned on and excited. Now I'm wondering if maybe..."

"Holy shit. You think Stacy poked holes in the condoms she gave you?" she exclaimed.

Jack shrugged. "We all knew that girl was batshit crazy. And she did want to have sex all of the time."

Ugh. The reminder of that trashy blonde being intimate with Jack was stomach-turning.

"Whatever she may or may not have done isn't important now," she said. "What does matter is that I'm pregnant, and I'm not sure what to do about anything. So can we just stay focused?"

This had to be one of those moments when the fates laughed directly in your face, right? Be careful what you wish for and all that stupid crap? You wanted to be a mother? *Bam.* Here's your baby. Was there a reason she couldn't find love and marriage first?

And the kick to the nuts of all this? The father of her baby just announced he was going back to riding bulls and risking death every weekend because it was awesome.

"Here. Take a seat, Mel. You're looking a little woozy." Jack guided her to the chair. "Okay. Now, I know this may sound like another jackass question, but are you positive you're pregnant? After all, it's only been over a month since we first had sex."

"I'm pretty positive. I'm late and I took a test." Three tests, actually. "Of course, there is the slightest, ever so slightest, possibility that I could just be late and it was a false positive. I have an appointment with my doctor tomorrow."

"Good. That's good." He took her hand and tugged until she looked him in the eye. "I hope you know that no matter what the results say, it'll all be good."

"It will?" Hope swelled in her chest and the sheer panic that had ridden her all day began to ease.

"Yeah." A twitch began at the corner of his mouth and slowly spread until his smile widened and that excited light returned to his eyes. "Yeah. Fatherhood wasn't something I had given any thought to. But a baby. Wow. That's wild."

Wild. That was one way to describe it.

"I'm scared, Jack," she admitted and bit her lip. "I wasn't planning on a baby either. Hell, I was planning on moving across the mountains. What will we do?"

"Before we start putting the cart before the horse and all that, let's just take it one day at a time. Once we find out for certain, we'll go from there."

"You'll come with me? To the doctor?"

"Sure. Of course. I have to ask for the time off, which may be a problem since we haven't told anyone about us. A baby will kind of blow that secret."

As if she hadn't given time to that very thought. While she had been worried about Jack's reaction, she had also been worrying about her brother's. He was gonna kill them for certain. Jack first, then her, then he'd go back and make mincemeat of whatever was left of Jack.

"I like your first idea better," she said. "One day at a time. Let's just get through tomorrow first."

"Look at me for a second, beautiful." Jack tilted her chin up then cupped her face in his hands and smoothed his thumbs over her cheeks. "There is no one on this planet I would want as a mother of my child than you."

Tears welled in her eyes. "Really?"

"Hell, yeah." He chuckled. "Looking at you right now, knowing you may be carrying my baby, you are so sexy right now."

"I am?" There was that Cannon charm that made her believe she was the most amazing woman on the planet.

"Yeah." He adjusted his belt buckle to make room for the growing bulge behind the fly of his jeans. "The thoughts I'm having about you right now…"

She rose and smoothed her palms over his chest, wrapping her arms around his neck. "Well, I had been planning on feeding you some dinner. There is a lasagna in the oven."

"You know, I had noticed that something was cooking when

I came in the house. Smells delicious. I would've mentioned something sooner, but I got a bit distracted."

"I understand." She batted her lashes. "I could turn the heat off and just let it keep warming in the oven."

He slid his hands over the curve of her butt and squeezed, pulling her against his pelvis. "Darlin', show me the way."

Giddy laughter echoed down the staircase as they raced to the bedroom.

Maybe, just maybe, everything was going to turn out all right after all.

Chapter Eight

MELODY'S TEETH CHATTERED as if they were castanets with the constant *click-click-click* echoing in the tiny exam room of her OB/GYN's office. Why was she so nervous?

Duh. She knew why. Just as she already knew what the test results were going to be before the doctor confirmed them. She was pregnant. A truth she felt from her toes to every single strand of hair on her head. There was no other possibility.

Jack slid his arm over her shoulders and took her right hand in his, giving it a squeeze. "It's okay," he murmured. "It's going to be okay."

"Who are you trying to make feel better, you or me?"

He issued a self-deprecating chuckle. "Both, I guess. I just want you to know that no matter what, I don't want anything to change between us."

Don't want anything to change between us.

Right. He kept saying that. But what did that mean?

Nothing would change. So, what, baby or no baby they were going to keep on dating? Keep their relationship smooth and easy with no thoughts toward a long-term commitment?

Yes, she understood that their relationship as it currently stood was new, but for how long was "new" new? At times she felt as if she were a father of a daughter in the 1950s, wanting to know what the boy's intentions were. A perfectly valid question she had every right to ask at any time. And she would. Just as soon as she stopped being a chicken shit. If Jack confirmed that she was only a friend with benefits, she'd die. Melt to the floor and slither away into a hole and die.

A light knock on the door made her straighten with a start. The door opened and the passive face of Dr. Wheeler appeared. She closed the door behind her and set her clipboard and papers on the counter.

"Well, kids," Dr. Wheeler addressed them, although Melody knew the doctor had just turned forty. The doctor's lips stretched into a big smile. "Congratulations. You're having a baby."

"Holy shit," Melody exclaimed on a rush of breath. Thank goodness she was already seated, for her knees would have buckled for certain.

She knew it. *She knew it.*

Jack dropped her hand and he seemed to sway on his feet. "We're having a baby. We're having a baby," he mumbled then smiled at her with such brilliance it was blinding. "We're having a baby, baby."

He swept her into his arms and cuddled her to his chest as her arms wrapped around his middle. She squeezed him so hard, the pearl buttons of his shirt dug into her cheek. Tears fell from her eyes and soaked through the cotton.

She was finally going to be a mother. With her dating history, she should have known her journey to motherhood was not going to be of the traditional route. With Jack now in her life, she hoped that her future was going to be nothing be lollipops and rainbows.

"Based on my calculations," the doctor said. "Your due date

should be about the end of April. We'll get you scheduled on the books for your next checkup. As long as everything is normal, I'll only need to see you about once a month until the third trimester. With your health, Melody, I don't foresee any complications, but we always like to be certain. In about twenty weeks, we'll schedule you for your sonogram."

Melody hoped that Jack was listening because she was only catching every other word. *She was having a baby.* Appointments, sonograms, prenatal vitamins, birthing classes. It was as if the doctor was the adult in a Charlie Brown cartoon and all the information was one big *mwah-mwah-mwah.*

Before she knew it, Melody was standing in the hallway outside the exam room with a packet of information and instructions and a box of sample prenatal vitamins.

"How are you feeling, darlin'?" Jack asked while rubbing his hand up and down her back.

"I don't know. My brain can't seem to focus on a thought for more than half a second."

Jack chuckled. "I hear you. I feel like I took a tumble off my horse and am seeing stars. Let's go back to your house and talk things through."

She reached for his hand. "When we get there, can you just hold me for a really long time?"

"Of course, sweetness." The blue of his eyes heated and he brushed his thumb over her cheek before raising their clasped hands to press a kiss on the back of her knuckles. "I'll hold you for as ever long as you need."

"Thanks, Jack." She blew out a breath. "Let's go, then."

They entered the waiting room of the doctor's office and Melody jerked to a stop with an almost comical gasp of horror. Good God, what fresh hell was this? Her worst nightmare had come to fruition, live and in all its high-definition glory.

Mark was wedged into one of the slim waiting room chairs and was flipping through the pages of a magazine as Gabrielle sat next to him, chatting with Rafe, who sat on her other side.

Wait. Rafe? What in the hell were the three of them doing at her doctor's office?

Her loud gasp had Mark lifting his gaze. He did a double take when he spotted her staring at him with mouth agape. "Melody?"

"Hey," she drawled, unable to say more than that as her brain refused to cooperate. "I…a…wha…Rafe?"

Gabriella laughed as she rose to her feet and pushed a lock of hair behind her ears. A pink flush raced over her cheeks. "I know this may look weird. I guess it is a little weird. But Rafe is here for support. You see, I'm having a baby."

Melody felt her jaw drop open. "You're kidding? Right?"

"Nope." Gabriella giggled and her hand fell to her belly. "I'm due in March."

"No way. That's—that's crazy. But so exciting." She pulled Gabriella into a hug and the two jumped up and down with joyous laughter. "I didn't even know you were trying to have a baby."

"We weren't, really. It was just one of those if it happens it happens, if it doesn't it doesn't things. Looks like it was meant to be."

Melody turned to reach out to her brother to give him a congratulatory hug and froze when she saw him staring over her shoulder with a dark expression pulling down his brows.

Jack. Right.

Crap.

"What is Jack doing here?" Mark asked and his eyes narrowed on her with laser-like focus.

"Ah, well." She swallowed hard. Where oh where to begin.

"Oh my gosh," Gabriella exclaimed and pointed at the box of vitamins in Melody's hands. "No way. Melody? No way!"

The heat rose in her cheeks and a fine layer of sweat broke out over her upper lip. "Um…well…"

"What is Jack doing here?" Mark asked again in a low tone she recognized as his "Be careful how you reply" authoritarian voice.

After several more failed attempts to utter a coherent word, Gabriella squealed and embraced Melody. "No way. No way."

Rafe rose to his feet and folded his arms over his chest. "What am I missing?"

"She's pregnant, silly," Gabriella gushed. "This is so great. We can be pregnant together."

Mark also got to his feet and took a menacing step toward Jack until they were practically nose to nose. "I'll ask one more time. What is Jack doing here?"

The muscles in Jack's jaw twitched and his nostrils flared.

Okay. Here it was. Time for the big reveal.

"I'm the father," Jack announced just as she sucked in a breath.

The air caught in her throat and she sputtered as the rest of the room fell silent. Three sets of eyes widened and they froze as if they had stared Medusa right in the face.

Melody froze along with them. The blood rushed in her ears and her eyes dried, afraid to even blink and disturb the moment of stillness.

Rafe was the first to crack. He grunted and winced as if he had watched one of those juvenile videos where a guy was hit in the groin because they were doing something stupid.

The sound set off Mark, whose jaws worked open and shut for several moments before he reared back and growled, "You son of a bitch."

He pulled his arm back, his fist clenched tight, as Rafe grabbed hold of Mark's shoulders and Melody jumped between her boyfriend and her brother. The rest of the lobby erupted in chaos as patients took cover and the receptionist reached for the phone to call the police.

Rafe pushed Mark into a chair while Melody scooted Jack to the other side of the room. Given that the lobby was maybe twenty feet across, that didn't give them much room to maneuver.

"No, no." Gabriella waved at the receptionist, who watched them with alarm on her young face. "We're good. No need to call the police."

A nurse barreled through the door separating the lobby from the examination rooms. "What is going on out here?"

Gabriella answered, "Brother, ex-boyfriend." She pointed at each man and ended with Jack. "Baby daddy. We just heard the happy news."

The nurse looked perplexed for a second until a sparkle winked in her eyes and she nodded. "I see. All right then, Mrs. Webber. The doctor will see you shortly. In the meantime, all of you." She pointed to the door. "Out."

"Come on, honey." Gabriella lifted Mark by the arm. "Let's get you some fresh air."

Mark glared daggers and his nostrils flared like one of the bulls Jack rode as Melody sighed and led the way outside.

The sun hit her in the face, blinding her for a moment. Spots danced in her vision, providing the perfect filter for her to turn to her brother and unleash the words that had failed her earlier.

"Yeah, see," she began with her eyes still closed tight. "Jack and I started dating about a month ago. And because it's new, and we are still learning about each other, we didn't want to say anything to the family. But by circumstances not entirely in our control, I am now carrying his child," she finished with a bright smile, hoping that any bad feelings her brother could be harboring would vanish in a blink.

Mark made a face as if he had just eaten the vilest thing in the world. "Carrying his child. I don't want think about my little sister having sex."

Melody pointed at Gabriella. "Hello, McFly. You think I like knowing how *that* happened?"

"Okay, you two." Gabriella stepped between them with her hands raised. Over the last year she had become well versed in managing the two siblings. "Let's be adults about this."

"Damn, I wish I had been recording this the whole time," Rafe said with his phone in his hand.

"Rafe," both girls shouted.

"What? No one is going to believe how painful this is," he said.

"Knock it off." Mark swatted at Rafe, trying to capture the phone.

"I don't know why you think this is so funny, Rafe," his sister said. "If you think about it, Jack has kissed both your sister *and* Mark's sister *and* both of you two's girlfriends." She tilted her head and frowned. "Actually. That is really twisted."

Melody groaned and dropped her forehead in her hand. And they said small-town life was simple.

"Everyone, just calm down." Jack raised his hands palms out. "Let's focus on the positives. Congratulations, you two, on your upcoming bundle of joy." He reached for Melody's hand and looked at Mark with the most serious expression on his face she had ever seen. His voice was low and husky as he addressed her brother. "Look, Mark, I care for your sister a great deal. And she is going to have my baby." The seriousness fell and he laughed. "Yeah. You're gonna be the uncle to my child. Ha-ha. I can see how that might put a burr in your britches. Nonetheless, we are all going to be one happy family, so just lay off the big-brother machismo, got it?"

Mark resettled his cowboy hat on his head. The brim cast a shadow over his eyes, but his flaring nostrils and the snarl to his lip was more than visible as he leaned closer and growled, "This isn't over, Cannon. Not by a long shot."

"Yes, it is," Melody said. "Can't you be happy for me?"

Mark grunted and paced back and forth as his gaze darted around, finally landing on the trio of nurses who stood at the plate-glass window of the doctor's office with their noses pressed to the pane. He turned in her direction. From underneath the brim of his hat, his brown eyes were flat with disappointment. "I can't think of anything right now. To say I'm in a state of shock is an understatement. I can't… I can't right now."

"Mark?" Melody said as he turned his back to her.

He was walking away? Really? Her big brother was walking away from her during the one time when she wanted his support the most?

Mark tugged his wife by the hand and led her to the office door. Gabriella turned around and gestured with her free hand as she mouthed the words, "I'll call you later."

Rafe followed, but stopped to give Melody a quick squeeze. "Congratulations." He leaned in and whispered in her ear, "If you need me to kick Jack's ass at any time, call me." He scowled at Jack before winking and following his sister.

A light breeze kicked up, but Melody swayed in the wind as if she were on a boat out at sea with the sails being buffeted by a tremendous gale.

She was prepared for Mark to be shocked. Pissed off, even. But the look of disgust that tinged his disappointment cut her to the bone.

How could he just walk away from her like that? As if she were nothing but a bit of manure stuck to the bottom of his boot? As if she wasn't his flesh and blood who had stood by his side his entire life?

Tears filled her eyes, and the entrance to the doctor's office blurred to the point where she saw nothing but gray. Shivers raced over her arms and a cold seeped into her bones that the hot August sun couldn't penetrate.

"Melody."

It was the husky, pain-filled tone in the sound of her name that made her open her eyes to the sight of Mark standing before her, his lips pinched tight.

"Come here, kid," he rasped and hauled her into his arms.

The heat of his embrace and the scent of his aftershave caused her knees to buckle as she promptly burst into tears.

Back and forth he rocked her in his arms, murmuring nonsense words and cooing sounds just like he used to when she was a small girl and needed comfort. This was the big brother she knew. This was the man who would fight anything and anybody to defend her. Even if that person was herself.

On a logical level, she knew Mark wasn't going to completely turn his back on her. Their bond was too strong. But for a moment, for those precious moments, the thought of not having him at her back was the same as if she had gone through an amputation and lost one of her limbs. He was her rock, her anchor. When all else in her life was going to hell, Mark was the one sure thing she could always count on.

Just as he could always count on her to be strong and stand on her own two feet.

"You should probably get back to your wife." Melody stepped away and swiped the back of her wrist over her wet cheeks. "She needs you."

"And you need me, too. We'll talk later," Mark rumbled and ran his hand over the top of her hair. "Love you."

"Love you too."

The shadows still graced his eyes, but the line of his lips softened as he kissed her cheek then turned. He didn't even glance Jack's way as he went back into the office.

Okay. So maybe he wasn't entirely ready to embrace her relationship with Jack. But she was willing to give him time.

"Hey, Mel." Jack turned her to face him and lifted her chin. "I'm sorry you got caught between your brother and me."

"I know it's not your fault. Mark probably would've had the same reaction no matter who it was who knocked me up."

"Hey." He gave her shoulders a little shake. "I'm not just some guy who knocked you up. I care about you, Mel. A lot."

He leaned down and pressed a soft kiss to her lips. A kiss of comfort and tenderness that banished the last of the chill from recent events.

"Come with me," he said and guided her to the passenger seat of his truck.

As he climbed behind the wheel, he glanced her way and flashed a secretive smile.

"What?" she asked. The afternoon had been filled with one shock after another. At this rate, she didn't think she could survive any more surprises.

"You'll see."

"No." She groaned and rested the back of her head against the seat. "No more surprises. I'm pregnant. Gabriella is pregnant. I can't take any more."

"You'll like this one." He chuckled and then fell silent. The rest of the drive to her house he remained quiet but for the occasional hum along with the radio while darting secretive glances her way.

"That secret squirrel look is starting to creep me out," she grumbled. "What is it already?"

"Patience, darlin'. Patience." He parked in her driveway then ran around the front of his truck to open her door before she managed to work the lock. He took her hand and led her through the side gate to her backyard. "Follow me, sweetheart."

He brought her to the little five-foot by five-foot shed she only visited to get out the lawn mower. Given that her backyard usually resembled a small jungle, it was obvious she didn't frequent this portion of the yard often. Since the Armstrongs did most of the entertaining, why did she need to break her back maintaining a lawn only she would see?

"I was saving this for the future, but I want to give it to you now," Jack was saying and glanced pointedly at the grass, nearly two feet tall. "It was too big to hide in the flatbed of the truck and I figured there was no way you'd find it in the shed."

"Ha ha. Funny. What is it?"

"Just a second."

It was difficult to remain impatient with him when he was so adorable with that light of expectation in his eyes and the delighted curve of his smile as if he were about to reveal a great treasure.

He made her wait outside the shed door as he opened it, then he covered her eyes and led her inside the tiny structure. The scent of gasoline and potting soil tickled her nose and set off around of nausea. Dear Lord, please don't let the morning sickness kick in. It would be a shame to ruin Jack's surprise by gacking all over the place when he was being cute.

He pulled his hands away and sang, "Ta-da!"

Leaning against the cobweb-strewn wall was a big white box with a picture of a mahogany crib on the side.

"Is that what I think it is?" she asked.

No way. He didn't.

"Yep. It's a crib."

She looked at him in surprise and tears filled her eyes for what felt like the millionth time that day. "You brought me a crib?"

"I brought the baby a crib. Where the baby is going to sleep is important. And I wanted our baby to have the best."

"You brought a crib?"

Jack laughed and pulled her into his arms. "I told you. I'm excited about this."

"I don't know what to say." She wrapped her arms around his neck and sobbed. "I'm sorry. I don't know what's wrong with me. One second I want to cry my eyes out and the next I want to jump you and ride you like a pony."

"Darlin', you can ride me like a pony any time." He laughed and leaned in.

Melody met him halfway and poured all the emotion and gratitude she felt for him in her kiss.

So his surprise wasn't a marriage proposal or a declaration of eternal love. But in her opinion, it was the next best thing. He was by her side and showing his commitment to their little family.

"Thank you, Jack. Thank you, thank you, thank you." She peppered his whiskered cheek with kisses.

"My pleasure. And don't worry about Mark." Devilish intent colored his smile. "I'll take care of him. Don't you worry."

Chapter Nine

J ACK PAUSED JUST inside of the mudroom of the Armstrongs'
house and peered through the doorway into the bustling
kitchen as if he were a peeping Tom. Figured everyone who
lived on the ranch would choose that morning to eat breakfast
together.

The morning tradition of a big family breakfast had changed
once some of the hands started shacking up with their girls, and
Greta's waffles lost the power to lure them out of a warm bed
with a willing woman spooned along their side. Apparently all it
took to rouse everyone at such an early hour was Nic's aunt
Jacquie's apple-cinnamon crepes and homemade croissants with
raspberry jam.

Damn. That buttery-flaky goodness did smell good. Too bad
his stomach felt as if it were running a CrossFit obstacle course.

It was probably in his best interest to wait to confront Mark,
but how in the hell was he supposed to sit across the breakfast
table from the man as if nothing had happened? The air between
them was as bad as a dustup after a stampede. If left unchecked,
someone was going to get trampled.

Fuck it. Just get 'er done.

He rolled his head to the left then right, blew out a few short breaths, then adjusted his belt buckle before stepping into the kitchen.

Mark sat in his usual spot at the far end of the massive kitchen table next to Trey. That meant Jack had to walk past Ben, Colby, and Faith as they sat discussing a list of places they wanted to visit on their upcoming weekend away. He sidled behind Nic's chair as she played thumb war with Adam over the last sausage on a platter and gave Nic's aunt Jacquie a tight smile as she said hello and flipped a crepe in the pan.

Gabriella stood by the center island with her coffee cup poised at her lips. Over the rim of the mug, she watched him pass, her eyes growing wide.

Jack came to a stop across the table from Mark who kept his focus on the plate of crepes and home fries before him. "Mark. Can I talk to you outside, please?"

"I have nothing to say to you," he replied, pushing the pieces of potato around the plate.

Okay. So he was still going to be as prickly as a porcupine. "Well, I have something to say to you. Step outside, please."

"What's going on?" Trey asked, watching them with his blond brows drawn into a frown.

"Nothing," Mark replied.

"Mark," Gabriella said in a clipped tone. "Go outside."

Mark shrugged and continued eating.

Fine. He drew in another breath. "For your sister's sake, you will want to come out and talk to me."

"Leave my sister out of this. This has nothing to do with my sister."

"Of course it has to do with Melody. She's having my baby."

There was a cacophony of gasps and the *clink-clank* of forks hitting dishware. Even baby Marta who had been cooing in Greta's lap, fell silent as all eyes in the room turned toward him.

"Melody is pregnant?" Greta all but shrieked. "With your baby?"

"I…" He looked to Mark in question. "Didn't you tell everybody?"

Mark closed his eyes and sighed. "I didn't say a word."

"Rafe?" He glanced at the cowhand, who shook his head.

Well. Shit.

Jack adjusted his belt as the heat of embarrassment burned a hot trail up the back of his neck and across his cheeks. "Right. So yes. I have been seeing Melody, and she has become pregnant."

"Fine." Mark wiped his mouth with a napkin and threw it over his breakfast and then stood. "Let's take this outside."

The tip of Jack's ears continued to burn as he followed Mark out the back door. Stellar. This was going to be one of the most stellar moments in the Sprawling A Ranch history.

Everything he had planned to say to Mark was lost in the breeze once they were outside on their own. Mark stared him down as he slapped at his pockets until he found what he was looking for in the shirt pocket over his chest and pulled out a pack of gum. Still staring at Jack, he slid two sticks out of the pack and unwrapped them before shoving both in his mouth.

Okay. It was going to be on him to start. "Sorry about that back there. I figured you had told everyone already. Or that Gabriella told Greta and so on down the line."

Mark continued to stare and chomped away at his gum.

"Right. Let's just get to it," Jack said and slapped his hands together. "What is your problem with me?"

Mark blinked once and then twice. "I don't have a problem with you."

"Are you certain about that? Sure, we needle each other now and again. Crack jokes at each other's expense. I think you're too uptight sometimes, and you probably think I'm not uptight enough."

"That's about right." Mark nodded.

"So whatever dislike you have about me, don't take it out on your sister."

Mark huffed and shifted his weight from one leg to the other. "It's not like that. It's just—she's my baby sister, man. Look, you're a decent guy, Jack. You're a damn fine cowboy. And you're family here. But Melody is my baby sister. And to find out that you two have been sneaking around—it hurts. I thought she trusted me."

"It wasn't that she didn't trust you. We just wanted to make sure that we were a 'we' before we announced anything to anyone about our relationship. Going from friends to lovers can be a tricky thing."

Mark winced. "God. Lovers. That's another thing. Who knows how many women you've been with."

He might have taken offense to that, but the man was having to cope with his little sister's sex life. He could afford to cut him some slack. "If I had to guess, I would say it's more than Colby but way less than Ben."

Mark blinked and a surprised smile worked at the corner of his lips. "Maybe. Maybe."

"In all seriousness, Mark, I'm going to do my best to do right by your sister. And the baby." He glanced off at the sunrise and gathered his thoughts.

Melody put on a good show about being the harassed little sister, but everyone knew how much she looked up to her big brother. The best thing Jack could do at that moment was spill his guts about his feelings and make sure Mark stayed on Melody's side.

"Melody…" Jack sighed and rubbed the back of his neck.

"Melody is way out of my league. Don't for one second think that I don't know that. She's a hell of a woman. Beautiful, smart. If she wasn't your sister, I would have taken a chance and asked her out a long time ago. But it wasn't until recently when I started to think of her as a woman. A sexy woman."

"Jack," Mark said on a warning growl.

"What I'm saying is, I'm lucky to be with her. She's great. And going to make a damn fine mother."

"Hmmm," Mark grunted in a way that was either an all-right or a we'll-see. He followed with a nod and settled his hands on his belt. "So I guess with the baby coming, you're done riding bulls, huh?"

"What?" He blinked with confusion. "Why do you say that?"

Mark's left eyebrow took a trip up north. "Don't you think this might not be the best time to be risking your life?"

"Oh, well, no need to worry about that. I've got at least a good year or two I figure before I have to retire. And riders have babies all the time. There are a lot of guys in the show with families." Of course, some of those were surprise babies from one-night stands, but still.

Mark rocked back on his heels. "And Melody is okay with you riding?"

"Oh yeah. She's all for it. Real supportive. She's super excited about coming out with me this weekend."

Mark chomped some more on his gum and nodded. Breaking his dark gaze, he scanned Jack from the top of his head down to his boots. "That's what she said?"

"Yeah." Although, the way Mark phrased the question and the curious squint of his gaze made him question that belief. He raced back through his memories of all the times he brought up competing and the upcoming rodeos and only remembered Melody smiling and telling him how happy she was for him.

"Yeah. She's real excited."

"Hmm." Mark grunted. "Then I guess you still plan on competing in Ellensburg."

"Damn straight. Hometown crowd and all. How can I resist?"

Mark nodded. "Well, good luck. Oh, and I'm obligated to tell you that if you hurt my sister, I will kill you."

Jack remembered when Mark told Rafe the same thing when he had briefly dated Melody. At the time, the fellas thought it was hysterical and a stereotypical big-brother thing to say. But now that Mark's serial-killer stare was nailing him right in the eye, there wasn't a thing that was funny about the way his nuts shrank into his body and his blood ran cold. The dude was serious. Hurt Melody and become fertilizer.

"Look, Mark." He swallowed against the goose egg–sized lump in his throat. "I can't promise to be perfect, but I'm gonna do my damnedest to make her and the baby the happiest people on the planet."

"I'm holding you to that, Cannon," Mark said on a low growl. The gold flecks in his eyes sparked and reminded Jack of a mountain lion lying in wait to pounce on their prey. "I'm holding you to that."

Chapter Ten

THE GOLD BUCKLE Club at the Ellensburg Rodeo was fit to burst by the time Melody arrived. For a pretty penny, memberships were available to join the fairground's booster club where members rubbed shoulders and dined on refreshments as they worked out the latest agricultural deal while the rodeo competitors poured their blood, sweat, and tears into their sport outside the Western saloon–style building on the north end of the arena.

Melody's tiny teacher's salary did not allow for the luxury of affording the annual dues, but with Greta home with her newborn, Melody was able to attend as Trey's plus one and have a front and center seat to watch Jack ride.

That was a good thing, right? Showing her support. Cheering loud and hard as her boyfriend was tossed like a ragdoll in a tornado. There was nothing for her to be worried about, after all. He was a professional. Sure, he was hurt once before and almost died. That did not mean he was going to get hurt again.

Dear baby Jesus, please don't let him get hurt again.

The Melody she had been prior to Jack laying that first kiss on her wouldn't have thought twice about the risks he was about to take. Well, she'd still be concerned, but only as a friend. And when it came time for him to ride, she would have been among the rowdiest of his fans.

Now he wasn't just her friend. He was the father of her baby and quickly becoming the love of her life. The stakes were now personal and she was struggling to connect to that carefree girl she once was.

Anxiety, hormones, and the scent of grilled meat mixed with a heady dose of drugstore perfume made her stomach pitch and roll as she pushed through the crowd in search of Trey. There were so many men in cowboy hats to wade through, the rodeo might be over by the time she found him.

"Melody, that is you," Adam's mother, Rebecca, said as Melody passed by her. Melody had been so focused on looking each man in the face, she didn't notice the older woman waving at her until she was almost right on top of her. "It's good to see you."

"Mrs. Maguire." Melody leaned in for a hug. "It's good to see you, too."

"It has been ages." She gestured to her family, who had taken up residence near the bar. "You know, we really should start up some of those old traditions again. It's the only time I see anyone in town on a regular basis. I think for the next Harvest Festival we should bust out that old buckboard and take a good old-fashioned hayride to Martinez's orchard."

"That would be great. We always had so much fun on those hayrides."

"Angus," Mrs. Maguire addressed her son. "Do you remember where that old wagon is?"

"I think it's in the garage with the dirt bikes. You know, I remember those times too." He winked at Melody. "First time I ever kissed you was on the way to the festival."

"Don't let your wife hear you say that," Melody said. "She's always hated that I was your in-between girl."

Oh yes, there was even a Maguire on her list of boyfriends past.

But she had been young then, and Angus a handsome nineteen-year-old whose girlfriend had been pushing him for a bigger commitment. He wanted to sow his oats and date other women before he was tied down in marriage, and Melody had been that oat.

Although at eighteen, she had been more of a woman-child than a full-on adult who hadn't yet understand the nuances of a serious relationship. She might not have been savvy enough to identify what had brought down Angus and Emily's relationship, but when Melody realized Angus was still in love with his high school sweetheart, she gave him a kick in the ass and pushed them back together.

"Emily's long over that now," Angus said. "Most of the time. Except in the fall. She does get a little twitchy when the leaves turn color."

"Uh-huh." Melody nodded. "Sounds like she's long over it."

Hamish Maguire, the patriarch of the Maguire clan, appeared at his wife's side and handed her a glass of wine. "Here you go, dear."

"Thank you." She flashed Melody a sheepish grin. "I normally don't indulge, but Travis and Zach are competing in the cow milking competition. Oh, I know my heart will be in my throat while they're out in the arena. I know they're grown men, but they are my babies."

"I understand how you feel. Jack's competing too."

"I thought I saw his name in the program," Hamish said. "I mean, how many Jack Cannons can there be?"

"He is one of a kind."

"Oh?" Mrs. Maguire's brows rose and her expression

changed from nervous to intrigued. "Do I detect a crush, Melody Webber?"

"I wouldn't say a crush, necessarily. We've been dating for a little while now."

The older woman bounced on the toes of her sneakers in delight. "That's wonderful. I do hope things work out for you."

Melody curled her fingers into her palms and resisted the urge to rest them on her belly. "I'm hopeful."

"Melody. Melody. Over here."

Above the crowd, Melody spotted a hand waving in the air. The crowd parted, revealing Gabriella standing at the fence next to Trey.

"It was nice catching up, Mr. and Mrs. Maguire. Good luck to you," Melody said and joined her friends where they had saved space closest to the action.

"We were wondering where you've been. How are you feeling?" Trey asked, giving her a big hug. "And congratulations."

"Thank you. I'm doing fine. At least, the baby is doing fine. Not a whole lot for it to do right now but float and grow. Me, on the other hand…" She snorted and glanced around in envy at the other patrons downing their refreshing cocktails. "I really wish I could drink right now. I swear, I'm ten thousand times more nervous than Jack is."

"Well, he is a pro at this," Gabriella said. "It's not his first rodeo."

Melody and Trey stared at Gabriella in silence as her joke died a death as fun as a cow patty on a golf course.

"What?" Gabriella shrugged. "I thought that was funny."

"City folk," Trey muttered with a shake of his head.

"Here we are, ladies." Mark appeared behind them with two glasses balanced in his hand. "Ginger ale for my girls."

"Thanks, Mark," Melody said and took a sip, desperate for

something wet to hit her dry throat.

"Good afternoon, ladies and gentlemen." The blast over the loudspeaker made Melody jump and slosh soda down the front of her shirt.

This was it. The rodeo was starting, and with it, Jack's return to the ring.

In the grandstands, all spectators were focused on the hillside behind the Gold Buckle Club where members of the Yakima Indian Nation began their annual descent to the arena floor. Dressed in their traditional Native American clothing and headpieces, the tribe paid honor to their past by entering the valley on horseback as their ancestors had done for the years long before white settlers had entered the territory.

With the action occurring behind the club, those inside the building watched the progression on the large screens in the arena. But Melody scanned the grouping of cowboys clustered against the stalls, preparing for the opening ceremonies. Bull riding was scheduled for the beginning and end of the rodeo, and the competitors were wasting no time in their preparations.

"Where is he?" she murmured, searching, searching, searching.

Amongst the blue and red cotton shirts, a flare of royal purple flashed in the sunlight. Jack.

He was so handsome in his purple long-sleeved shirt and black leather vest. A helmet rested under right arm and his bull rope was slung over his shoulder. Tools of his trade, but on Jack they were oh so sexy accessories that added to his masculine charm.

Jack had drawn the fifth slot in the first round of riders. With a maximum ride of eight seconds per rider, it was going to be his turn in no time at all. Did the man look as if he had the slightest bit of nerves? Not a bit. Even from across the distance of a few hundred feet, his smile was huge as he joked with the other competitors and while standing at attention for the national anthem. To see him so relaxed helped lay her own nervousness to rest.

Okay, maybe "to rest" wasn't quite the right choice of words, but at least the chills that made her hands shake had ceased.

The last note of the "Star-Spangled Banner" still hung in the air and the final sponsor horse had barely cleared the arena when the first gate opened and man and beast barreled out into the open field.

The bull bucked and kicked into the air as the rider resembled a piece of taffy flapping in a hurricane-force breeze. The cowboy lasted for all of three seconds before he slid sideways off the bull's back and tumbled to the ground.

But the bull wasn't done with his performance and charged the rider and the barrelmen, twisting and turning in search of an area of escape. His nostrils flared and he lowered his head as he ran straight at the fence of the Gold Buckle Club.

Intellectually, Melody knew that where she and the others stood was safe and heavily fortified, but with those blazing beady eyes and the sharp pointy horns coming right at them, she tensed, ready to jump out of her seat and race for the door.

Before the bull connected with the paneling, two pickup men headed off the animal and diverted his attention to the open gate, where he trotted out as if he hadn't a care.

In the blink of an eye, another gate opened and the second bull and rider shot into the arena.

With her heart still racing, Melody imagined the ginger ale in her hand was made up primarily of whiskey and downed three big gulps.

"Ahh!" She choked on her soda and about jumped out of

her skin when a weight landed on her shoulder.

It was Trey. His fingers curled around her shoulder. "Relax, Mel. It's fine. Everyone's fine. We're all good."

"Are you saying that for my benefit, or are you worried about Jack, too?"

"Jack? I'm not worried about Jack. He's tough. He can handle falling on his ass." Trey spoke a good game, but the edges of his smile trembled ever so slightly. He cleared his throat. "I'm—I'm gonna get a beer."

That's it. Rub it in that you can use a bit of liquid medication to settle your nerves.

"Wait a minute," Gabriella said, and brought the rodeo program closer to her face. "That's my brother's name I see there. And Adam's."

Mark sputtered around the neck of his beer. "I thought you heard about that."

"Cow milking?" she asked. "What the hell is that?"

He chuckled. "Well, it's pretty much like it says. One man on horseback chases down a cow, ropes it, and tries to hold it still while the other man runs out and tries to squeeze some milk into a bottle. Cow milking."

Gabriella blinked at him. "And my brother agreed to do this?"

Mark coughed and brushed his finger alongside his nose. "Not exactly. He and Adam lost a bet. It would've been Colby and Ben. I thought you saw them practicing the other day."

"Rafe told me he had those baby bottles to give to me as a present. Remind me never to accept a bottle from Rafe or Adam ever."

"Ladies and gentlemen," the announcer said. "Welcome from Benton City, Brody Carter."

Brody Carter. That meant Jack was going to be the next to

go.

In Melody's hand, the program turned into a crumpled scrap of paper as she watched through the slats of the chute as Jack climbed onto the back of the bull.

What was it that he said again? He wanted a bull that drew to the left, or was it the right?

The top of Jack's helmeted head bobbed up and down as the bull shifted its stance, trying to buck him off before they began.

Doomsday. That was the name of the bull. Just once she'd like to see a bull named Snowdrift or Applesauce.

"Welcome back, Jack," Melody caught the tail end of Jack's introduction before the gate whipped open and Doomsday came charging out.

"Oh my God. Oh my God. Oh my God." Melody counted off each second with prayers to the Lord as Jack's lean body cracked back and forth like the end of a whip. Dust flew into her eyes but she didn't blink the entire time his thighs gripped the animal.

The buzzer. *Where was the freaking buzzer?*

Nothing registered in her brain. Her focus was so tuned to Jack, nothing else existed. No crowds, no cheering, nothing except the blur of Jack's purple shirt and the brownish-grayish hide of the bull twirling in front of her.

In a blink, Jack was off. He stood in a cloud of dust with his arms raised, pumping his fists in the air.

Wait. What happened?

Melody was jostled to and fro as Trey and Gabriella on either side of her gave her hugs and cheered in her ears.

He made it. He rode. He was walking—okay, limping—out of the arena, but he made it.

She squinted, trying to detect by sight alone if his limp was worse than normal.

But he was okay. Jack survived, and he even covered, scoring in the low 80s. That was good. Maybe his return to the rodeo wouldn't be so bad, after all.

The crowd gasped and Melody's gaze was diverted to the next rider in the arena, who was curled up in a ball in the dirt. Bullfighters surrounded him, trying to turn the bull's attention in their direction as a few crewmembers ran out to assist the downed cowboy. Scooping him under their arms, they carried his limp form out of the arena.

Oh no. This was bad. This was really bad.

Chapter Eleven

*Y*ES. *YES. YES!*

Jack slapped the hands of his fellow competitors as he exited the arena. He was back. He was back and better than ever.

Well, maybe not better than ever. He winced as the adrenaline subsided and the pain in his ankle radiated up his leg. Okay, maybe that landing hadn't been his best. But he covered the bull. That was what was most important.

"Hey, Jack." A svelte blonde in a red halter top and tight denim shorts ran up to him and threw her arms around his neck. "It's so good to see you again. Where've you been, sugar?"

"Oh, Brandy."

"Sandy."

"Right, Sandy. Hey. Nice to see you too." Untangling her arms from his neck reminded him of those plastic bands that slapped around the wrist. Get one half off and the other side snapped into place.

"What are you doing later? Going to listen to the band?"

"Ah, maybe. Depends on what my girl wants to do."

"Girl?" Her red lips pouted. "You have a girl?"

"I do. She's real sweet."

"Oh. Well, that doesn't mean we can't hang out afterward

and party." She pressed a gloss-slicked kiss to his cheek. "See ya later, handsome."

Wow. Well. Guess Rodeo Jack was still a hit with the ladies.

He hobbled toward the dressing room with a swagger to his step, rolling and flexing his muscles to work the kinks out of his system.

"Good ride there, Jack." Sterling greeted him coming out of the dressing room. "You looked pretty good."

"Feeling good, too. Can't believe I've been gone for so long."

"Don't get too comfortable." Sterling slapped the helmet tucked under his arm. "Prepare to have the bar set high."

"Good luck."

Once Jack stowed away his gear, he ambled toward the sports medicine trailer. The interior was nice and cool as he stepped into the tiny space where the athletes could receive a little TLC before and after their rides.

"Jack." An older gentleman with salt-and-pepper hair and wearing a belt buckle as big as his head greeted him with a huge smile. "Welcome back, son. Good to see you."

"Dr. Jenkins, good to be back."

"How was your ride?"

"Eighty-two, thank you very much. I think I landed on my ankle wrong. Can you give it a look?"

"Of course, my boy. That's what we're here for. Jack, meet Kathleen."

Jack turned his attention towards a pretty blonde who stepped out from behind the curtain separating one of the ends of the trailer. "Hi. Please to meet you."

She shook his hand with a firm and efficient grip. "Nice to meet you, too. Hop up on the table and let's see what you got going. Did I hear you say it was your ankle that was bothering you?"

"Yes, ma'am."

Her lips twitched at his polite address but she didn't reply. Obviously, she'd been around enough cowboys to know he didn't mean to make an indirect comment about her age but was simply being polite.

Kathleen poked and prodded at his ankle while asking him questions. She straightened with a sigh and adjusted her ponytail. "It's tender, slightly swollen, but not broken. Let me get some tape and I'll patch you right up."

The door to the trailer opened and Sterling poked his head in the opening. "Hey, Cannon. Someone is looking for you. She claims to be your girlfriend. I don't know if I believe her. She's too cute to belong to you."

Melody's adorable face appeared over Sterling's shoulder.

It was on the tip of his tongue to announce that Melody wasn't just his girlfriend, but he kept the words at bay. Although a few people knew about their upcoming bundle of joy, it was still early in Melody's pregnancy, and they didn't want to jinx the baby by breaking some unknown baby taboos and announcing the news too early to the world.

But the idea that she was *just* his girlfriend felt wrong. Melody was quickly becoming more, much more to him. He wanted more from their relationship, but he didn't want to push her for too much too soon. After all, they were already putting the cart before the horse by getting pregnant before professing any words of love.

"Hey, beautiful." He waved her over. "Come inside."

As Melanie approached, he noted the concern in her eyes and how her lips were pinched tight with fear as she watched Kathleen work on his ankle.

"Jack, are you okay?" She rubbed her thumb over his cheek.

"Is this blood?"

"What?" He reached up and touched his face. On his fingers was a sticky, red substance. "Ah, nah. That's just lipstick."

"Lipstick? What?"

"It's nothing. And my ankle is fine," he said, changing the subject away from why there was lipstick on his face. "Just a little twist. Nothing a little time and a few minutes off my feet won't cure." He reached out and took her hand. "No need to be worried."

"I'm not going to listen to you. You are a man who wants to do what he wants." She turned toward Kathleen. "How is he, really?"

"He'll be fine. Just needs to take it easy for the rest of the day." She held out her hand. "I'm Kathleen."

"Hi. I'm Melody."

"Is this your first time to the rodeo?" Kathleen asked.

"Oh, no," Jack replied. "Just her first time since we've become a couple. Melody hasn't gotten yet used to the fact that her man will come home with some bumps and bruises."

"From the scars on your leg, I'm guessing it's been more than a few bumps and bruises for you," Kathleen said.

"Well, you do get a little scrape now and then." Jack winked. "Seriously, Melody. I'll be fine." The worry had yet to ease from her eyes.

"Have you been doing this long?" Melody asked the woman.

"For a few years now. This is my first year touring with the sports medicine trailer. Don't worry." Kathleen placed a hand on Melody shoulder. "I speak from experience. He's fine."

"Thanks," Melody said with a slight tremor of relief in her voice. Then she cupped Jack's cheek. "You did so well. We're all proud of you."

"I can't tell you how great it feels to be out there again. With my friends watching, that just made it all the better. Thank you, Miss Kathleen." He hopped down from the table and took Melody's hand to press a kiss on her knuckles. "Now, darlin', let's head out and find the others. I'm starving and there's a brisket sandwich out there with my name on it."

"Trey and Mark are talking shop at the Gold Buckle, and Adam and Rafe are out at the general store trying to talk the salesgirls out of the twenty-five-cent limit on the penny candy. But the girls are saving a table for us."

"Fantastic. Lead the way, my love."

Chapter Twelve

"CONGRATULATIONS, JACK." TREY held up his bottle of beer in salute. "Well done, man. Well done."

The rest of the party guests cheered in celebration of Jack's third-place finish at the rodeo. Third place. Not too shabby for his first time officially back on the bull.

The bonfire was blazing at the Sprawling A Ranch and a huge moon hung in the clear sky over the crowd of ranch hands and rodeo attendees who had come to celebrate the end of a successful weekend. Jack heaved a contented sigh, and the scent of grilled steaks and hot buttered corn filled his lungs. Life couldn't get much better than holding a frosty cold one in his right hand and his favorite girl in his left.

His decent finish in the show confirmed that he had what it took to get back into the game. And of course, the prize money was a much-welcomed benefit. He liked thinking of things to buy for the baby, and the extra dough went a long way to help with those plans.

For some reason the thought of unexpected fatherhood didn't terrify him as he would have imagined it might have had it been a few months earlier. In fact, over the last few days he had been caught staring out into the horizon daydreaming about little things, like teaching his son how to ride a horse, or his daughter how to rope her first calf.

He suspected the main reason for his excitement over the unexpected change in his life plan was due to the woman cuddled against his side. Being with Melody was better than anything he had dreamed of when he had allowed himself to fantasize about her in the past. Before, his visions had been about them tearing up the sheets. Now they included snuggles in front of the television and mornings spent playing footsies under the breakfast table. They were the types of moments that warmed a soul from the inside out and a cuddle that lingered long after the embrace ended.

Now that the rest of the world knew about his and Melody's relationship status, he took great pleasure in being able to pull her close in front of God and everyone and lay a kiss on her that was for mature audiences only. He felt her smile against his mouth as she giggled and nipped playfully at his lips.

"Mm…you taste like strawberries," he said. "I want to taste you all over."

She giggled again and hugged him tight around the waist. "Sounds lovely. But I do need to watch the time. It's starting to get late and I'll need to head home soon."

Home.

Uh. Recently, that word had started to rub him raw like a burr in his saddle blanket.

With him living on the ranch and Melody residing in town, they were close to their prospective jobs. But the next morning was Labor Day and right after that was the start of the school season, which meant late nights spent in Melody's arms were going to have to wait until the weekends. That was a reality that pained him more than being gored by a bull. He wanted her with him at night. He liked waking up and having her in his bed. And when the baby came, he didn't want to miss a single second.

Having her come live with him in the bunkhouse was a definite no. For three bachelors, the place was paradise. For a young family, not so much. At all. Never. And they were already cramped with Nic staying with Adam during the rebuild of the bakery and her home she shared with her aunt.

Of course, he could always move in with Melody in her little house in town, and he probably would. If she asked him. When it came to the possibility of them living in the same house, Melody's intentions were as empty as an apple tree in winter. Sure, their relationship had taken off like a stallion being chased by horse thieves, but they weren't the typical couple. Melody had to know that things were different with him. *He* was different.

He loved Melody Webber.

For the last few years, she had been right in front of him. But with her being Mark's sister and gaining the friend label early on, she had been hidden from his radar. Yes, he had always thought her beautiful and smart. Now that he had been with her on an intimate level, he discovered all the hidden qualities about her that he had quickly come to love. The way she lingered over her morning tea, or how she flipped her hair off her face as she laughed. He loved how she talked about teaching and her students, and the way she could cut her brother with a sassy remark but still retain the love she had for him in her voice all tugged at his heartstrings.

So yeah, the thought of her driving back to her house alone stung him like no other.

"Stay with me. Please?" he asked. "I'll even come help you set up your classroom after my morning chores are finished."

"It's your party. You should say."

"Darling, I'm just the label of the week. Come on." He took her by the hand and led her down the road to his bachelor pad.

"They won't even know we're missing."

"I think that not only would they notice, they'll know what we're up to, too. Don't be surprised if Mark comes pounding on the door any second."

He laughed. "You just proved my point. He and Gabriella skipped out about ten minutes ago. And by the way he was looking at her, they're about to get down and dirty."

"Ugh. No." She pulled a face as if she had just bitten into a lemon. "Why did you say that to me?"

"Just reminding you that your brother is a red-blooded man, too." He pulled her into his room and locked the door behind them. "Okay, woman. Get naked. Now."

"Ah, so that's how it is. You just looking for a booty call, Jack?"

"Not *just* a booty call. It's been a busy weekend. My testosterone levels are going crazy, and you are a beautiful, sexy woman who I have not had in my arms like I've wanted to for far too long. But if you're telling me you're getting sleepy, then I need to move fast."

"Is that so?" The words might have been said dismissively, but the tilt of her head and the sparkle in her eye were clear signals that the game was afoot.

"Yep. Don't make me hogtie you."

"Ooo. That sounds fun."

He cupped her face in his palms, brushing his thumbs over her petal-soft skin as he savored the taste of her lips and her sigh as she melted against him. Her hands gripped him by the belt, hauling him closer. He tilted her head to the side and trailed soft kisses along the line of her neck, inhaling her sweet floral scent.

"Oh, Jack," she sighed, and a shot of desire hardened his already stiff cock.

Torn between wanting to rip her clothes from her body to

take her to the floor like an animal and cherishing her like a delicate princess, he set about undressing her with hands that shook with need.

He tried his best to kiss and touch every inch of skin he revealed, but his control was rapidly slipping. "Lay back on the bed, darlin'."

He attacked his own clothes as if they were on fire, ripping them from his body and following her onto the bed before she even had a chance to get settled.

"Hey," she said. "I didn't get a chance to see you strip."

"Next time. I need my hands on you now."

He hugged her into the curl of his body and drank from her lips as his hands skimmed up and down her curves. Between her thighs, she was already slick and ready for him and he delighted in hearing her whimpers as he played with her sweet spots.

He painted her fingers with the juices of her pussy then licked them off. "You taste good, baby. I need more."

"I need you. I need you hard and hot inside me," she panted.

"Like this?" He plunged his fingers back inside her sheath.

"No. Your cock. I want your cock."

"How bad do you want me?"

"Bad, Jack. Please."

"Tell me, you naughty girl." He loved watching her as she grew wet and flushed in his arms. The sound of her begging was so sweet his back teeth ached.

"Dammit, Jack. Take me, you son of a bitch."

He chuckled and rolled her onto her side before he lifted her leg at the knee to slant over his hips and brush the tip of his cock against her folds. She sucked in a sharp breath.

Without the fear of pregnancy, they had agreed to forgo condoms. Having her wet heat surrounding his throbbing length was a pleasure beyond compare and he relished every second he took as he slowly slid his hard shaft deep into her body.

His eyes rolled back in his head as he groaned, "Damn, that's heaven right there, baby."

"More." She dug her nails into the shoulders. "I need more."

"Greedy, aren't you? I don't want to hurt you."

"You won't hurt me. I want it. I need it. Please."

He knew Melody could take whatever he dished out, but he hesitated due to the tiny life growing inside of her. It was an adjustment, getting used to the fact she had to share her body with somebody else.

But Melody wanted nothing of his tender touches. She rolled him onto his back, straddling his waist. He almost cracked a joke about having her ride him like a bull, but the look in her eyes stopped him cold.

There was a hunger there, almost a desperation and a fear as she raised and lowered her hips with wild abandon.

"Take me. Take me, Jack," she grunted. "Make me feel it."

This was a Melody possessed. Somehow in the blink of an eye, something had grabbed hold of her and turned her into a tigress on the hunt. What exactly she was seeking, Jack hadn't a clue. But it seemed as if she was trying to milk his very soul.

"What do you want, baby? Tell me."

"Make it hurt. I want to feel you for days afterward." She leaned forward and pressed her pink nipple against his lips. "Brand me. Brand me good."

"You want a ride? I'll give you a ride." He wrapped his lips around her nipple, drawing it deep into his mouth as he wrapped his hand in her hair and the other gripped her hip as he began to lunge and thrust inside of her body.

"Yes. Yes," she moaned.

Beneath him, his bed creaked and shuddered. The pace was frantic, and all too soon he felt that rising in his balls. She just felt too good. "Melody. I'm gonna come."

"Do it, come inside me. Make me yours, Jack."

Fuck. She knew just how to push his buttons.

Thank heaven she was right there with him. Her back arched as she let out a cry as her pussy squeezed around his shaft, drenching him in her cream as he filled her with his own. Together they lay, shattered and shaking as their orgasms washed over them.

Holy shit. What the hell just happened?

Melody collapsed on his sweaty chest and curled on top of him as if he were a mound of pillows, nuzzling her face into his neck. "Don't let me go, Jack. Please. Don't let me go."

With the little strength he had left in his arms, he held her tight.

"Never, darlin'. Never."

WELL, SHE GOT what she begged for.

Melody moved and stretched her limbs, stifling a groan as her muscles ached with each gesture. She couldn't fault the man. She had wanted him to take her hard so she could feel it for days, and that's exactly what he delivered.

She wasn't exactly sure what had come over her the night before, but fear and anxiety had been laying on her shoulders all weekend long like an old, wool poncho. Thick, scratchy, and just as oppressive.

It was one thing to know that Jack rode bulls, and another thing altogether to see it with her own eyes. To watch his body whip around like a ball at the end of a rubber band being thwacked by a paddle was one of the most frightening things she had ever seen. At any moment, she expected his body to break just as easily as that rubber band. Snap. Bang. Incapacitated or even dead in less than eight seconds.

And although Jack smiled and said he was fine, it wasn't until she had him warm and in her arms that she was certain he was physically okay. She needed undeniable proof that he was still strong, still capable of loving her, comforting her.

To her relief, he could. And he did. Several times during the night, in fact. Now she was going to pay the price for all that passion. But to know that Jack was the same Jack made the aches totally, completely worth it.

"God. I'm so fucking sore."

Confusion struck Melody for a moment as she didn't think she had spoken the words out loud until she realized she hadn't. Behind her, Jack shifted on the bed sheets and groaned.

"Jack?"

"Morning, baby doll. Damn. I forgot how much a weekend of riding takes out of me."

"Are you okay?"

"Nothing that a few hours of PT won't fix." With more grunts, he rolled to his feet and began to shift and roll his body and arms one way, then the other. Rolling his shoulders, he bent at the waist and a giant crack echoed in the room that made Melody wince.

"God damn," Jack groaned. "That feels a little better. I'm going to jump in the shower and hit some hot water on these muscles. Want to join me?" A tremor tinted his sexy smile.

"Not this time. I'll make breakfast and have it ready for you, okay?"

"I'll miss you." He shuffled over to her side of the bed and dropped a kiss on her lips before straightening with another moan.

Melody eyed his cute backside as he limped toward the bathroom. In the light of day, the swatches of bruises on his back and thighs were a tapestry of crimson, blue, and purple against his pale skin.

Her hands fell to her belly as her thoughts turned inward.

One rodeo. One weekend, and Jack was walking as if he were an eighty-year-old with a hip displacement. And he wanted to do fifteen to twenty rodeos a year? For how many years?

If he couldn't take care of himself, how was he going to take care of his family?

Chapter Thirteen

"OKAY BOYS, LET'S kick this show in the ass. The sooner you give me my championship belt, the sooner we can all hit the bar for a beer," Colton Proctor said, settling his hat on his head then reaching for his bull rope.

Jack and Sterling exchanged an eye roll then went back to preparing their gear for their own rides. Colton was always going to talk smack, they were always going to ignore him, and at the end of the day, it was skill and luck that got you to the top of the trophy stand.

"Ah. Fuck." Jack's joints cracked and popped as he moved into a series of stretches to loosen his limbs.

The physical therapy he did during the week leading up to the Puyallup Rodeo helped some, but his body wasn't bouncing back as it once had. He tried not to let it worry him too much, but to be free of that niggling thought that your body might give out at the worst moment was a hell of an advantage.

Cheers arose from the crowd as the next rider burst into the arena. Jack raised his gaze to the stands and scanned the section for any sign of Melody. He squinted and picked out Ben's huge figure about halfway up the grandstand. Faith stood to his left with Colby and Melody. The trio had taken the trip across the mountains with them so Melody didn't have to travel over the pass by herself. Ben mentioned something about taking Colby and Faith to some kind of cavern during the weekend. Jack didn't know what that was about, but Faith got really excited when he mentioned it. Funny, Jack didn't know they were into cave diving at all.

Jack focused on Melody and the way the late summer breeze played with her hair, dancing the long strands across her soft lips. She was stunning in her beauty, as always. But what worried him was the furrow on her brow.

In recent days, a worry line as deep as the Columbia River had formed on her forehead, and her eyes didn't sparkle as they once did. For a woman who was in a delicate condition, he often caught her watching him as if he were the one that was about to break.

Obviously, she was concerned about him. He didn't blame her. Bull riding was a dangerous sport. But he was a professional. This was his job.

From his observations of the female sex, he knew all the verbal reassurance he could offer wasn't going to ease her tension. Having been around the women of the Sprawling A Ranch over the last few years, he had learned that actions spoke way louder than words. All he needed to do was continue to do well, and in time, Melody would see that she had nothing to worry about. She was going to have to learn to trust him.

That meant kicking Colton's ass in the finals with the perfect ride. The trick was in the preparation. He double checked the straps on his red leather chaps and smoothed out the fringe. There were a few rhinestones missing along the ankles, but he still looked pretty sharp. At least in his opinion.

He looped his bull rope around the fence and began the process of rosining the rope. He lost himself in the rhythm of cleaning the poly and applying the sticky substance that would help him keep a good grip. The rattle of metal as the animals shifted their weight in the chutes, the drone of the announcers calling out the play-by-play all faded into white noise as his hearing homed in on the rasp of his glove creating friction on the rope.

"Cannon." He felt a hand slap him on the shoulder. "You're up."

Jack secured the rope then climbed into the chute. He had drawn a Brahman named Killer Wasp that had the reputation of a Tasmanian devil. The bull shuddered as Jack dropped onto his back, but the fit under his seat felt good, comfortable, as if the bull had been molded specifically for his dimensions.

"You got this, Jack." "Here we go, Jack. Here we go," his spotters called out.

Jack sucked in a breath, then another. In and out. In and out. He warmed up the rope with his hand to get it hot and sticky before setting his rope in place and tightening his fingers around the handle.

"We're ready when you are, Jack."

Jack raised his free hand and gave the nod. *Clang.* The chute opened.

One thousand one.

Jack leaned forward and drove the animal out of the chute.

One thousand two.

Killer Wasp straightened and galloped straight ahead.

One thousand three.

Turn, you son of a bitch.

One thousand four.

Turn. You're costing me points.

One thousand five.

About damn time. Killer Wasp turned into his hand and kept

spinning.

One thousand six.

A flash of red and white came into the viewfinder of his mask. Realization slowly dawned that he was heading headlong into a giant banner advertising Western wear strapped to the fence of the arena.

The bull charged and smacked his back hip against the wall, smashing Jack's leg into the barricade.

Fuck. Killer Wasp rolled and flung Jack to the ground as if he were a sack of potatoes. Two bullfighters stepped between Jack and the bull as a third rushed up to lift Jack under his arms.

"Can you stand, cowboy?"

"Yeah." Jack shook his head to clear his vision. "I think I got it."

"Watch out! Watch out!"

A hot gust of hay-scented breath seeped through the sleeve of his shirt a second before the bull ducked his head into Jack's side and tossed him into the air. The world spun in several rotations before he hit the ground with a puff of dirt and then it all went black.

Chapter Fourteen

"**H**OW IS THAT?" Melody asked Jack and fluffed the pillows underneath his left leg. She shook out a blanket and laid it over him, tucking him in.

"I'm fine, Mel. No need to fuss over me."

She had to fuss over him. If she didn't do something with her hands, she might do something crazy like strangle him or reach for the bottle of whiskey that was out in the boys' kitchen.

She didn't think her heart had slowed for one second since she watched the bull drop and flip Jack into the air as if he were a pancake. While his protective gear kept him safe from a concussion, his left knee had taken a beating and was bruised and swollen.

"He'll be fine," the doctor told them.

"He'll be fine," the other cowboys said as he was carried away in the arms of the bullfighters to the waiting medical team.

"I'll be fine," Jack said with a smile.

No. He wasn't going to be fine. Sooner or later his luck was going to run out and he was going to become injured to the point of incapacitation, maybe even death. How long did he think his body could hold out?

"You shouldn't be fussing over me like this, Mel. I should be the one fussing over you."

Ah, he shouldn't even get her started on that one. Yes, here she was carrying his child. Doing everything in her power to keep his baby safe. And what was the baby's father doing? Joyriding on two thousand–pound animals for sport.

Don't think about it. Don't think about it. If you do, the injury to his knee will be the least painful thing on his body.

"Jack, please do what the doctor said and rest."

"I will, darlin'. I need to be healed up for Pendleton this weekend. It's the hometown crowd and all."

Pendleton?

"You plan on riding this weekend?"

He blinked with surprise. "Of course. It's one of the biggest rodeos. And it's my hometown. I gotta go."

"Jack, you were almost killed yesterday."

"I'm sure it might've looked that way, but I was nowhere close to dying." He patted the space next to him on the bed. "Why don't you come here and snuggle with me? We can watch some *Monday Night Football* together."

Oh my God. He was serious.

Normally, she was the one who was all about live and let live, but fear for his future, *their* future, could not stop her tongue. "You know, Jack. I was trying to be supportive and keep an open mind, but maybe you need to rethink this competing thing."

"What do you mean?"

"I mean maybe you should stop riding bulls. If you really need to be a part of the rodeo, go back to your plan to be a pickup man. But stop with the bull riding."

"Melody, I don't understand. I thought you were all for this."

"I said I would try to keep an open mind." Her voice shook

as she remembered the sight of him flying feet over head across the arena. "I can't keep watching you almost die."

"I'm not gonna die, Mel. Hurt, sure. But I'm not gonna die."

"You can't make that promise. Look at you." She gestured to his knee. "What's next? Dislocated shoulder, concussion, scratches, bruises, broken backs. It's only a matter of time before something life threatening happens. And for what? Ego?"

"That's not fair." A red flush graced his cheeks and his nostrils flared. "I'm just a little rusty. I'm getting better."

"At what cost?" He wasn't understanding. Was he not understanding on purpose or was he really that unaware?

Did it matter? If he couldn't see the stress his riding was causing his relationship, then maybe she needed to take herself out of the equation.

"Jack, I can't... I don't think I can do this anymore."

He huffed out a breath and pinched the bridge of his nose. "I get it. A lot of wives and girlfriends can't watch their fellas compete. I understand. You don't have to come with me to the rodeos anymore if you don't want to."

"No. That's not what I mean." Her throat tightened. Was she really going to say it? "I don't think I can do this." She pointed back and forth at the two of them.

Jack stilled and his voice lowered as he asked, "What are you saying?"

"I'm saying." Damn. It felt as if she swallowed a baseball. "I'm saying that we—I have to decide on what's important. What's the best for everyone. There is more than just you and me to consider. This baby needs parents."

"I intend to be there for my child every step of the way."

"Right. You *intend*. And the next bull you ride may have different intentions. I can't count that you'll come home every weekend."

He shook his head and scrubbed both hands over his face. "Before you start making any rash decisions, it's been a long weekend. We're all tired. Let's just take a day to relax. Come sit by me and everything will be fine in the morning."

Fine. There was that stupid word again.

"Are you going to quit riding?"

"Mel."

"Are you going to quit riding?" she shouted.

"No," he barked and the muscles in his jaw bunched. "I'm a bull rider. It's in my blood."

Ah-ha. The clouds parted and the angels sang in glorious refrain. If she ever had a question about his priorities, they were now crystal clear.

Well, she had her priorities, too.

"Maybe you need to be the one to take a day and think about what's important to you, Jack. Seems like I have plans to make."

"Melody," he shouted.

As she fled his room, the creak of bedsprings and Jack's grunts and curses followed her down the hall.

"Melody!"

Even with a bad leg, he made it to the front porch by the time she hit the gas and sped away in a plume of dust. Despite her determination to not look, she peeked at the rearview mirror to see him tottering on his one good leg dressed only in his boxer briefs with his brows furrowed and his mouth drawn in a hard line. His devastated image wavered as tears filled her eyes.

"Don't cry," she muttered. "Do not cry. This is all on him."

Was she being irrational, running out like that as if she were on some reality celebrity housewife show? Maybe. Slightly. But she was right when she said they both had to think about their priorities. With the baby on the way, their wants had to change.

And she seriously had to consider the possibility of raising her baby on her own if something terrible were to happen to Jack. What if he became incapacitated to the point where she had two people to look after?

No. She was not wrong. They both needed time to think. And Jack needed to get his head out of the bull's ass. Decisions needed to be made and time was running short.

Chapter Fifteen

"J ACK, WAIT UP," Rafe shouted and ran around Jack to form a barrier between him and his Silverado.

"Rafe, get out of my way, man."

"You're going to see Melody?"

"Yeah." He had given her the night to cool off, but now it was time to talk, and if she wasn't going to answer his calls, then he'd damn well chase her down.

Rafe folded his arms over his chest. "No."

"No," Jack repeated. What the fuck? "Really? Get out of my way."

"No."

Jack frowned at the tall Latino. "Is this about me having to till that backfield? I told Trey I will get to it later on this afternoon. I need to speak to Melody."

"No, you don't. You need to give her space."

"What do you know about anything?"

Rafe rolled his eyes. "The walls of the house are thin. I can hear everything. Which is especially bad when you and Adam are both getting your freak on and I'm the only single guy in the house."

Damn. He was afraid somebody might have heard his and

Melody's argument.

"Melody is family to me now," Rafe said with a shift of his weight. "And you're causing strife to my family. I'm here to make sure you do things right by her."

"Is that so? Or is it because you still have the hots for my girl?"

"Shit, Jack. Don't be stupid." Rafe shook his head. "Do you know why me and Melody never worked out? It's because she was a rebound girl for me and she wanted to get back at Mark for leaving town for those few weeks without notice. It didn't take us long to figure out that we made better friends and there was never going to be anything more between us than friendship. And I love Melody like she's my sister, which is why I'm here to talk to you now. Why did you piss her off?"

"Piss her off? That's rich. We just have a difference of opinion, that's all."

"She wants you to stop riding, doesn't she?"

"Yeah."

"So why don't you stop?"

Jack felt his eyes bug out to the point that dust flew into them and made them water. "Riding is in my blood."

"What about Melody?"

"Melody... Melody." Jack sighed and stepped around Rafe to lean against the front of his truck. The ache in his leg was killing him. "I love her."

RAFE SETTLED HIS weight beside Jack. "You know the equestrian show that I used to work for? Right before I worked here? You've heard me talk about them."

Jack nodded.

"Family-run. Went back generations. And for Mr. Junglar, the show wasn't just in his blood, it was in his DNA. His very soul. It was what made the family *the* family. And if you ask the rest of the Junglars, they all felt the same way. But then one of his daughters was injured. She missed the trick, broke her back. Laid her out for quite a while, but when she was healed and her therapy was going well, her father expected her to get back on the horse. She didn't. She couldn't."

"She was afraid?"

"Yeah, I suspect that was part of it. She never would open up exactly as to why. I think also it was the risk. She wanted something else in her life besides the show. She wanted a family. She wanted a career that didn't mean her potential death."

Rafe gazed off into the distance with a dreamy look in his eyes. "You should've seen her on those horses. Beautiful. Brought tears to your eyes with how one she was with the animal. But for her, riding wasn't worth the risk of further injury. So she walked away. Old Man Junglar didn't take very kindly to that. To not be in the show was to deny their family. So he threw down the gauntlet. Ride or she was no longer a part of the family. She walked. He lost his daughter because she wanted something different. Because she had a new dream. Don't lose Melody because you can't find a new dream, Jack. Is riding bulls worth losing your family?"

"This is different. Your friend didn't want to take the risk. I'm willing to take the risk, because I know I'm good. I know these injuries are just because I'm getting back into the groove. Once I settle in, I'll be fine. I just need to make Melody understand that we can have a future together, even if I ride."

Rafe shook his head. "That's your choice. And your consequence." He stepped away from the truck and took two steps forward before pausing to say over his shoulder, "But you're not gonna find her at home."

"What do you know?"

"I might've heard from Gabriella that Melody was going across the mountains. She has an interview with one of the schools in the city."

"An interview? No. She turned that down."

"Maybe if you took a moment to talk to your girlfriend about things other than the rodeo, you would know that she might have reconsidered. But then, why should what Melody wants mean anything to you?"

The low blow bounced off him as if he were rubber as his mind struggled to process this latest bombshell.

Melody wasn't only planning on leaving Mission, but she wasn't even going to tell him.

He hobbled to the driver's side of his truck and climbed in. He needed to see her. Talk to her. Make sure this wasn't a big misunderstanding. Although why Rafe had any reason to lie to him, Jack didn't know.

He made the drive into town in half the time and slammed to a stop in her empty driveway. The house was silent as he let himself in. The only clue he had of where she may have gone was the calendar hanging off the door of her computer armoire. A purple circle was drawn around the date of her next doctor's appointments and right next to it in red ink was a time and address in the city.

How long had that notation been there that he hadn't seen it? How long had he been in danger of losing Melody and not even known?

Chapter Sixteen

"MAMA." JACK DROPPED his duffel bag on the front porch of his childhood home and wrapped his mother in a big bear hug.

"Oh, my boy." Brandy Cannon squeezed her son tight. "It's about time you came around to see your dear old mother."

Old? His mother looked every bit the blue-eyed, blond-haired rodeo queen she had been when she had been a child bride at age sixteen. Still, he did notice a few more lines bracketing her mouth and around her eyes than he remembered. But it had been well over a year since he had last seen his parents in person.

"It's been busy at the ranch. People coming and going. Then there was Trey's accident, and marriages, and babies. But I'm here now."

Her eyes twinkled as she smiled. "You're here now." She kissed his cheek. "I've missed you so much. Phone calls and video chats are just not enough."

She pressed another kiss to his cheek then glanced around him. "I thought you were bringing a girl? Melody?"

His gut clenched. "Yeah, Melody had some schoolwork come up. She said she's sorry she'll miss meeting you."

At least he believed she was sorry about not meeting his parents. Melody had always been the gracious sort, and her beef was with him, not his family.

Tension was still running high between the two of them, especially after finding out she was considering leaving town without telling him. Camping out in his truck in front of her house all day long until she returned that evening hadn't helped his temper either.

All intentions of discussing the matter like cool, rational adults blew to smithereens the moment he saw her sour expression as she climbed out of her car.

"You're taking a job in the city?" he had shouted. "Without even telling me? What about our baby?"

"Don't start, Jack." She turned her back on him to retrieve her overnight bag and slammed her car door shut. "The only person who's really thought about our child's future is me. All the cribs, and toys, and baby gear you buy will not replace a father if you die in the ring. I need to have a plan in place in case I need to raise my child on my own. I need to have security."

"You can't just leave and move across state."

"Nothing's official. I'm just checking my options." She opened the front door of the house and stopped him from following. "No. You're not coming in."

"Melody, we have to discuss this."

"Are you riding this weekend?"

"Of course I'm riding."

"Then we have nothing to discuss."

Bam. She slammed the door in his face.

He would have made the effort and beat down her door if her brother hadn't shown up at that moment to play guard dog. Fists hadn't been thrown, but there had been a whole lot of eye daggers tossed at each other.

Gabriella had been there too, and suggested it was best to give Mel some space. Although it galled Jack to walk away, he gave her some distance. Three days later, he was more anxious about his return to Mission than he was facing his next bull.

"Is that Jack I hear?" The deep booming voice of Robert Cannon echoed from inside the house. The man couldn't speak in a whisper if his life depended on it.

The shuffle and scrape of boots on the hardwood floor preceded his father's appearance in the hallway. Where his mother was small and curvy, his father was tall and lanky. His old man was a good twelve years older than his mother, having won her heart with the classic Cannon charm evident in his sparkling blue eyes and wide smile.

Robert pulled him into a big bear hug and jerked him across the threshold. "There's my boy. We've missed you, son."

"I've missed you too, Pops." He winced as he received a few more slaps on the back.

"Come in, come in. Take a load off. Tell us what's been going on in your life."

"Ha. I don't know where to even begin."

Stepping into the living room of his childhood home was like standing before a museum display dedicated to his life history. Along the walls hung eight-by-tens of his school pictures, along with team photos of when he played baseball. Along the mantel the trophies he had won as a youth gleamed with a freshly polished shine.

The crown jewels of the collection were the buckles he won for placing in the finals along the Columbia River circuit. Those beauties were laid out on purple velvet in the china cabinet next to those won by his mother during her rodeo competing days. There was enough gold and silver on those shelves to rebuild his Silverado three times over, which was why his mother was the keeper of his buckles. He'd like to think he'd never sell one of his precious buckles, but when his truck needed yet another repair, the temptation was strong to let go of at least one of his winnings.

With the weather clear, bright, and a glorious seventy-five degrees, the Cannons did what they had always done and settled in the backyard at the large patio table with the blue-and-white striped umbrella. His mother brought him a glass of lemonade and a slice of angel food cake she had waiting for his arrival.

"So what's been going on with you, Jackie?" she asked as she took her seat. "You said you had some exciting news."

"Yeah." He rubbed his neck. "Yeah. There's been lots of things going on."

"You know how excited we are you've been cleared to compete again," his mother said, beaming and patting his hand. "It's so good to see the Cannon name on a rodeo program again."

"For a while I didn't think that was ever going to be possible." He chuckled. "Can't tell if it's good fortune or dumb luck I happened to be at the right place at the right time."

"Talent, son," his father replied, emphasizing his point with a jab of his fork in the air. "It's talent that got you back in the arena. Let me tell you, we've got some fine bulls for you boys to ride this weekend." His father laughed and slapped his knee. "About a third of them are already scheduled to be heading out to Las Vegas for the championship. There'll be some good competition between us and Clay's outfit."

"Clay's got some pretty spirited animals, that's for sure," Jack said. "Damn, Mom. This cake is good."

"Just wait to see what we've got coming up from the ranch." A delighted smile curled Robert's lips. "We bred Homerun with a sweet little Angus a few years ago and they're producing quite the offspring. You should see some of them buckers."

"Oh, yeah?"

As his father filled him in on the latest news at the stock contractor he worked for over the last thirty years, he noticed his mother watch their conversation with her head going back and forth as if she were viewing a tennis match. The frown on her forehead deepened with each passing second until she slapped her hands on the table, drawing their attention.

"That's it?" she asked with disappointment. "Was that all of your news?"

"Pretty much." Jack shrugged.

"Jackson Justice Cannon."

Uh-oh. All three names. His mother was on the hunt for information.

"I was certain you had another announcement. That's why you were bringing Melody. I was expecting that you had proposed and were getting married."

"Oh." Heat raced up his neck that wasn't caused by the midday sun. "Uh, no. Melody and I are not getting married. But I do love her. I love her a lot." He paused to clear his throat. "And, well, we're having a baby. I mean, she's having my baby."

Stunned didn't begin to describe the absolute shock that froze on his parents' faces. Even the gentle summer breeze had died down and the birds ceased their chirping as the minutes ticked past.

It was his father who was the first to blink. "A baby? I'm gonna be a grandpa?"

"Oh my," his mother gasped. "Oh my. A baby. Yee-haw," she whooped and threw her arms into the air. She leapt from her seat and danced in circles before throwing her arms around Jack. "A baby. How exciting!"

"I'm glad you think so," he said, and forced a smile to his lips to match his mother's enthusiasm.

"Uh-oh. I recognize that look." His mother retook her seat, pulling her chair closer to his then grasped his hand. "What's going on?"

He stared so hard at the empty cake plate before him, the white crumbs blurred as if they were snowflakes in a shaken snow globe. "Melody doesn't like that I ride. She thinks it's dangerous."

"Of course it's dangerous. That's what makes it so exciting. I don't blame her for being concerned. When you're riding, I worry about you from dusk to dawn."

He looked at his mother in surprise. "You never told me that."

"Do I really have to tell you?" she drawled with sarcasm as thick as honey in her tone. "You are my baby. Anytime you're in danger, my hair turns gray with the stress. L'Oréal made so much money off me when you were riding full time. The minute you said you were done with the rodeo was one of the happiest days of my life."

Was she kidding? "Why didn't you say anything?"

She tilted her head and glared at him in the motherly version of "duh." "Because that was your dream. I'm not going to stand in the way of your dream."

"Dad, are you listening to this?"

Across the table, his father sat with the muscles in his face slack and his gaze lost somewhere in the distance. A bee buzzed over his ear, yet he didn't flinch.

The last time Jack remembered his father sitting so still and quiet was after the accident. It felt as if he had lost days while undergoing surgery. When the anesthesia had worn off and conscious thought reignited, he had spotted his father in the chair by the window. For the first time, Jack saw a man who was vulnerable, helpless, and uncertain of the future.

The moment Robert noticed his son was awake, however, the clouds had lifted and the confident smile reappeared as if his doubt had never existed.

Was that what was happening now? Was his father torn between his dreams for his son's future or the concerns carried by his wife?

"Pops, you're awfully quiet."

Robert shook his head as if waking from a dream. "A grandchild. That is something. That's a wonderful something."

"Thanks. But Melody wants me to stop riding. In fact, she's thinking about moving to the city if I continue."

His father frowned. "You said you love her, son. Do you?"

"Yeah. She's wonderful."

"Then you quit riding."

"I quit? Just like that?" Who *were* these people? His parents were rodeo people, twenty-four/seven, three hundred sixty-five days a year. They lived and breathed the rodeo competition and culture. And they were telling him to up and quit?

"Yes. You quit riding. Just like I quit when you were born," his father replied.

"Wait. What?" Jack sat there as if he had just had a bucket of ice water dumped over his head. "I don't understand," he mumbled through frozen lips. "Bulls? When did you ever ride?"

His father chuckled and sat back in his seat. "I was riding bulls since I was thirteen years old. How do you think your mother and I met? She was barrel racing, I was riding bulls. It was a love born amongst the sawdust and manure."

"I thought you met at the rodeo because you were working stock."

"I went to work for the Montecito's once you were born. We realized once we held you in our arms that you needed both parents with you. Family. Stability. Working the circuit was not stable. And I would have missed out on so much of your life if I had continued."

"But for my entire life, both of you have gone on and on about how proud you are of me riding."

"Of course we're proud of you, sweetie," his mother said. "You're our son. You're doing what you loved. Who wouldn't be proud of you? But it's not because you were riding bulls. It's because it was you and we love you."

"I still don't understand."

The rodeo was in their bones. How could they be happy if he wasn't a part of it? "All my life, all I've ever heard about is rodeo. It's all you've ever wanted me to do."

"That's not entirely true, Jack." His mother clutched his hand in hers. "It's just what this family's always done. But it's not all that we want you to do."

He sat there with shock skittering through his system as he tried to digest the fact that his parents saw in him more than just a bull rider.

"Jack," his mother said in a stern voice. "Is that why we haven't seen you in so long? Because you weren't riding anymore?"

His throat closed and his eyes began to water. Unable to speak, he nodded.

"Oh, Jack." His mother got out of her seat and hugged him. "I don't know if I should shake you or hug you. We love you. We love you, no matter what."

"I just—I just want to make you proud," he choked out.

"Son." His father paused until Jack met his gaze. His father's eyes were filled with tears. "Do you have friends?"

Jack nodded.

"Are you working in a job that you love?"

Jack nodded, this time with much more enthusiasm.

"Then we're proud of you, son."

Jack nodded again and swallowed past the lump of stupidity lodged in his throat. "I've missed you. I've missed home."

"And we've missed you." His mother kissed him on the cheek. "All of you. Don't you ever doubt that we're proud of you. Now, let me get supper started and you can tell me all about my new grandbaby."

Jack grew lightheaded and slightly dizzy as a weight came off his shoulders. Deep, deep down he knew his parents loved him. But for years he believed they might love him just a little less because he hadn't succeeded as they had planned. With that burden obliterated, hope gave him the strength to move mountains.

It didn't matter if he won the competition the next day. Hell, he didn't even need to place. The only thing he needed were the smiles and the love of the people in his life. And when it came to obtaining everything he could ever desire, there was one last person he needed to make amends with and convince there wasn't a shiny buckle in existence that was more important than her.

Chapter Seventeen

T HE CROWD OF fifteen thousand held their collective breath, and some stood in wide-eyed terror with hands over their mouths, as they stared at the broken man lying in the dirt of the arena floor.

The overcast sky blended with the blues and denims worn by the spectators, creating a dull backdrop against the red flashing lights of the ambulance as it pulled into the arena.

Jack watched the scene unfold through the slats of the stalls. His hands tightened over the railing and his heart felt as if it was about to crawl out of his throat.

"Move," he murmured. "Come on, Sterling. Move."

It all happened so quickly. One second, Sterling was looking good. His pockets were off the back of the bull, and he was driving the action at a steady pace. Then Jack blinked and Sterling was off and being dragged through the dirt with the tail of his bull rope tied around his leg.

From what Jack could tell, it appeared as if Sterling's shoulder had dislocated again and thrown his weight off balance. With the tail of his rope hanging over his thigh, he got tangled up like the string of a kite trapped in a tree in a hurricane-force wind.

The pickup man had been able to ride up alongside the bull

and detach the rope, freeing Sterling, who tumbled across the ground like a tumbleweed.

The bulls trapped in their stalls next to Jack shifted their weight and tossed their heads, sensing the tension in the air. These were competitors as fierce as the men who rode them, and they didn't take kindly to be pinned in for so long.

Jack's eyes felt as if they were about to shrivel up and fall out of their sockets from being kept wide open for so long. He didn't want to miss any sign of movement from his friend.

Between the gaps of men on the field, Jack watched as paramedics lifted Sterling onto a gurney. They strapped him down tight and covered him with blankets before loading him into the back of the ambulance. The click of the doors closing echoed across the hushed stadium.

The ambulance started its journey to the gate, and one of the pickup men came up to the group of cowboys standing with Jack.

"He's breathing. Conscious," the pickup man said. "But he can't move. They're going to take him in for X rays."

He was breathing. That's a good sign. Conscious was good, too. But the most important thing was he was alive.

"Cody," the show manager announced. "You're up."

Just like in show business, the rodeo had to go on.

All around him, people jumped into action. Riders strapped on their gear, stockmen loaded the animals, and rodeo officials attempted to get the crowd primed for more action.

One of the bullfighters waved at Jack and ran over, grabbing his wrist and dragging him into the arena. "Don't worry, folks. Sterling is going to be just fine. We got the best paramedics taking care of him as we speak. Now, while our riders are resetting, I realized we haven't properly welcomed home Pendleton's favorite son, Jack Cannon. Y'all might remember

Jack had that nasty fall a few years ago, but look at him now. Back in action and ready to kick some bull ass."

A smattering of applause broke out and grew around the grandstands in a wave. In seconds, the crowd got to their feet, cheering him on.

The bullfighter raised Jack's hand over his head and said to him through a tight smile, "It's all show business, son. Remind them that this is just entertainment."

Jack forced a smile and waved at the audience. Just entertainment. Maybe to the organizers. To the men who put their lives on the line, this was their everything. This was their life and their death.

And Jack recognized this was one of those moments when you acknowledged whether you either loved it beyond your love of self, or if you just went home.

"Okay, kid. Time to get out of harm's way." The bullfighter shoved him back toward the open gate a second before the stall opened and the next rider exploded through the opening.

Cody Haynes was one with the beast, hanging on for the full eight seconds before jumping off and landing on his hands and knees in a plume of dust. The crowd erupted in cheers while Cody ran in the opposite direction of the bull with his arms stretched out, drinking it all in. Now there was a young man who loved riding more than he loved himself.

Jack's heart tugged with remembrance, with that memory of being indestructible. And hot on its heels was the remorse that the sensation wasn't as strong as it used to be.

As the applause faded away, Jack swore he heard his name being shouted on the wind.

"Jack. Jack!"

Wait. That was his name. Shouted by a woman.

He looked around as the shouting of his name grew closer.

He looked up and his breath caught in his throat.

Mother Nature saw fit to have the clouds part and allow the sun's rays to hit the woman standing in the grandstands above him. The top of her dark hair reflected in the sun like a halo of golden red. The corner of her lips trembled as she smiled and gave him a little wave. In her dark eyes was both concern and adoration. For him.

Melody.

His knees turned to mush and he about sank into the dirt with relief. She had come. She was there.

Her smile grew and she placed her hands over her belly. Her lips formed the words, *We love you.*

He lifted his hand and swirled his fingers, acting as if he caught her words in his palm and pressed them against his chest. *I love you, too.*

Right there, standing in the grandstands in a swirling sea of spectators, was his world. That's what he would give his life for. That woman. His Melody.

A tap on his shoulder about made him jump out of his boots. "Cannon, you're up."

Shit. He still needed to ride.

Didn't he?

Jack closed his eyes and reached out with his senses. The sound of the cheering crowd, the clatter of metal on metal as the chutes opened and closed, the huff of the animals as they snorted through their wet noses. He sucked in a breath, tasting that strange tang of cow manure, kettle corn, and fried foods on the back of his tongue.

He settled his helmet on his head, absorbing the weight on his scalp as he fitted the strap under his chin. Strapping on his glove, he flexed his fingers in the stiff and sticky material.

He slapped at his chaps as he stalked toward the stall. The

jingle of the bell on his rope faded with the white noise of the crowd. He glanced back at Melody and caught her eye. He raised one finger in the air.

Her brows formed a V-shape for a second until he shook his finger once more.

One. One more time.

Her gaze softened and her shoulders relaxed. With a nod, she pressed her fingers to her lips and threw him a kiss.

He climbed into the chute and settled himself in his seat, handing the tail of his rope to the flankman. "Good luck, Cannon."

Jack gave the nod. The gate opened.

One thousand one.

Last ride, old boy.

One thousand two.

Melody loves you.

One thousand three.

Oh, you fucker. You're gonna turn left on me now?

One thousand four.

Keep your focus.

One thousand five.

If we have a boy, do you think Melody will let me call him "Tornado"?

One thousand six.

She'd probably trounce me harder than this bull.

One thousand seven.

This was it. This was it.

One thousand eight.

The horn blew and Jack let go of the handle, leaning into his shoulder. He kicked his leg over the back of the bull and rolled across the dirt as the world spun wildly between the slats of the visors on his helmet.

The crowd erupted in cheers as Jack stood, much the same way as Cody had done a moment before, arms out with his face up to the sky. Only one thought was on his mind. Melody.

He raced for the opening in the fence line. Ripping off his helmet, he tossed it who knew where then stripped off his gloves and tossed them behind the soon to be forgotten helmet. He raced up the ramp to the grandstand, searching frantically for his girl. He grew dizzy with relief as he spotted her racing toward him. She jumped the last few feet, leaping into his arms as he crushed her to his chest.

"I love you, Jack," she sobbed against his neck. "I love you so much."

"I love you too, baby. You mean more to me than anything."

"I'm sorry."

"No," he said, dropping kisses to her hair. "I'm sorry for letting you think you weren't the most important thing to me."

"Okay, you should be sorry about that." She slapped playfully at his shoulder then placed her hands on either side of his face, pressing her forehead to his. "You're sitting second, Jack. I'm sorry you didn't win with your last ride."

He tipped back his head and roared with laughter. "You're wrong there, darlin'. I did win." He hauled her into his arms. "I won it all."

Chapter Eighteen

M ELODY OPENED HER front door and blinked into the afternoon sun. As the spots in her vision cleared, the handsomest man she knew was smiling at her, holding a bouquet of wildflowers.

Jack handed her the bouquet. "The love of my life."

When he said corny things like that to her, she couldn't help but giggle as delightful tingles shot through her body. Whatever she had believed love to look and feel like was a total farce compared to what she experienced with Jack. Never had any man treated her with the love and kindness Jack had shown her.

"Thank you, sweetie." She turned and walked into the kitchen to put them in a vase with water, replacing the ones he had given her the week before. She loved how he brought her a different variety each time.

"Ready to go?" he asked. "I believe a cheeseburger was on the menu for today."

"God, yes. I can't stop thinking about cheeseburgers. And onion rings. And lots and lots of ketchup."

"Then let's get to it." He took her hand and led her outside, pausing for a moment as she locked the door behind them.

With the house secure, she followed him down the steps

toward his truck and pulled up short in the driveway. Instead of his Silverado, however, a black four-door sedan sat in the driveway.

"What is this?"

"It's my new ride."

"What?" What strange alternate reality had she stepped into? "What happened to your truck?"

Jack shrugged and escorted her to the passenger side. "It wasn't getting very practical, especially with the baby on the way. Where was I going to put the car seat?"

True. But… "You loved that truck."

Jack grinned and tucked her into her seat before walking around the front of the car then settling in beside her in the driver's seat. "I love my family more." He rubbed his thumb at the frown lines between her eyes. "Don't worry, Mel. This is good. It's taken a little bit for me to get used to the handling, but I can live without the Silver Bullet."

"I have to say, Jack. I'm—I'm stunned. And a little sad. And clearly have no idea what's going on."

He laughed and patted her on the knee. The little sedan started up with the roar of a baby kitten. "It'll be okay, darlin'. We'll get through it together."

He had made so many sacrifices for her. His rodeo career, now his truck. Sometimes she wondered if she asked or expected too much. But then he'd smile at her with that flash of a dimple and without a speck of remorse in his eyes. The man was amazing.

"I love you, Jack."

"I love you more." He gestured to the side of the road. "Hey. Look at that."

She shifted her gaze to where he pointed and sucked in a gasp. Right there, glinting in the late autumn sun glittered a red and white for sale sign with the word "SOLD" cutting across the lettering in bold font.

"The Emmert house. It's sold." She placed her hand on her chest over the ache that ignited beside her heart.

"Why are you so sad?" Jack asked.

She dabbed at the corner of her eyes with the sleeves of her cardigan. "I'm sad that it sold. But I'm also happy. I hope that whoever bought it will make great memories."

A devilish glint colored Jack's smile and he turned into the driveway of the house. "Let's take a closer look."

"What? We can't. It's private property."

"It just sold, so it's in transition. It'll be fine. It's perfectly legal."

"You are totally making that up. You're going to get us arrested for trespassing."

"You're being silly." He edged the car down the lane to the front porch. "Nobody's gonna arrest a pregnant lady."

"There's always a first."

As the engine died, Melody sat frozen in her seat and stared through the passenger window at the grand old home.

Upon closer inspection, the siding was much more worn than it had appeared from the street. But the porch was gorgeous, and the windows looked to be the original glass from when the home was built.

Jack came around and opened her door. "What you waiting for? Let's explore."

"I don't think I can," she said even as she allowed him to pull her from the car. "I'm afraid I'm going to disturb the natural presence and disrupt something in the force, bringing a curse down on our heads or something."

"Your imagination sometimes." Jack shook his head and took her hand to lead her up the front steps.

As she stepped onto the porch, a warmth seemed to surround her, almost as if the house was opening its arms and enveloping her in a great big hug. She crept up to one of the windows and cupped her hands against the glass to peer inside. Hardwood floors fanned out as far the eye could see and a grand staircase ran right up the center of the house.

To the right, she spotted the entrance to what could have been a formal living room. To the left, perhaps the family room and what looked like kitchen cupboards.

"Jack. I think they remodeled the kitchen." She turned around and her jaw about hit the floor.

Before her, Jack was down on one knee with a sweet, but slightly hesitant, smile. In his palm rested a red velvet box.

On an intellectual level, she understood what was about to happen. But at that moment her brain was fried, the synapses barely connecting as she stared at him wide-eyed.

"What's going on?" she muttered.

Jack chuckled. "Melody Ann Webber. Will you do me the honor of becoming my wife?"

Funny how that even though they had a baby on the way, they had never discussed marriage. They had both just kind of gone with the fact that it was a given that they'd be together forever.

But now Jack was making it official. He was asking her to marry him. With her brain scrambling to take a mental picture of that exact moment to keep with her forever, she found herself unable to speak.

Jack's eyebrows rose. "Melody?"

"Yes," she said with a crack in her voice. "Yes. A thousand times yes."

He wilted as if he had been held up by strings that had been suddenly cut by a pair sharp scissors. Then he stood. "For a second you had me scared there, darlin'."

Before he finished his sentence, she jumped into his arms and laughed with joy as he spun her around the front porch.

"I guess that leaves one more thing," he said as he set her back on her feet.

"There's more?" she exclaimed. "Oh, Jack. You and your surprises. I don't think I can take anymore."

"You'll like this one." He reached into his pocket and withdrew a set of keys. Jangling them before her eyes he said, "Wanna see your new home?"

Okay. Now she was certain she wasn't functioning at full mental capacity.

"Jack Cannon. What did you do?"

He laughed and the dimple reappeared as he brushed past her to unlock the front door. "Welcome home, sweetheart."

No. No way.

"You didn't," she said as her heart pounded and her knees threatened to buckle. Impossible. "You couldn't."

"Of course I could. I just took what I've been saving to fix up the truck and used that to make an offer." He slapped his hands as if dusting them off. "House is ours."

Tears cascaded down her cheeks. "Oh, Jack. I can't—I can't believe it. I don't deserve it."

"Baby doll." He took her into her arms and smoothed her tears away with his thumbs. "You more than deserve it. You deserve the moon and the stars, and I'm gonna do my best to get them for you."

"I just—I can't." The tears turned into full-on sobbing as she collapsed against his chest. "You've given me so much."

"You're kidding, right?" He placed his hands on her gently swollen belly then leaned down to kiss the bump. "You're giving me the world."

This had to be a fantasy, right? The man of her dreams. The house of her dreams, all bathed in the yellow glow of the summer sun.

"I can't believe this is happening." Her cheeks ached from smiling.

"Believe it, darlin'."

"I love you, Jack. House or no house, I love you."

"I know. That's what makes you so sweet, Mel. And why I'm gonna take my time with this."

She let loose a shriek as Jack lifted her into his arms and approached the doorway to the house. He paused for a moment to give her a lingering kiss on the lips before they crossed the threshold.

Also by Anna Alexander

Men of the Sprawling A Ranch Series

The Cowboy Way

The Marlboro Man

To Have Faith

Sweetest Kisses

Eight Seconds to Forever

Heroes of Saturn Series

Hero Revealed

Hero Unleashed

Hero Unmasked

Hero Rising

Cavern Series

A Night at The Cavern

Only at The Cavern

Elite Metal Series

Bound by Steele

Adamantium's Roar

Thallium's Submission

Vibranium's Truth

ABOUT ANNA ALEXANDER

Award winning author Anna Alexander is the author of the Heroes of Saturn and the Sprawling A Ranch series. With Hugh Jackman's abs and Christopher Reeve's blue eyes as inspiration, she loves spinning tales of superheroes finding love. Anna also loves to give back and has served on the board for the Greater Seattle Romance Writers of America as chapter president and on the committee for the Emerald City Writers Conference.

Sign up to receive news about Anna's latest releases at
http://eepurl.com/Q0tsz

Anna welcomes comments from readers.

Website

annaalexander.net

Facebook

facebook.com/pages/Anna-Alexander/282170065189471

Twitter

twitter.com/AnnaWriter

Newsletter

http://eepurl.com/Q0tsz